D.W. CROPPER

Bonechillers

About the Author

D. W. Cropper works in a library, and is married to a librarian, but he isn't a librarian himself. He is actually an accounting clerk, which is an unfortunate occupation he fell into by spending entirely too much time writing weird stories. Most everyone who knows him, including co-workers and family, agree that he is quite a weird person, which may or may not explain why he writes these stories. But many suspect he actually writes what he writes because he doesn't like kids. In fact, he never liked kids when he was a kid himself, and now he spends entirely too much time making up weird stories to frighten them in the hope that they'll be kept awake all night and act cranky toward their parents in the morning, as their parents were once kids too and shouldn't escape unscathed either. Oh, and he has a dog, so you should like him for that.

To Write to the Author

If you wish to contact the author or would like more information about this book, please write to the author in care of Llewellyn Worldwide and we will forward your request. Both the author and publisher appreciate hearing from you and learning of your enjoyment of this book and how it has helped you. Llewellyn Worldwide cannot guarantee that every letter written to the author can be answered, but all will be forwarded. Please write to:

D. W. Cropper
℅ Llewellyn Worldwide
P.O. Box 64383, Dept. 0-7387-0758-9
St. Paul, MN 55164-0383, U.S.A.

Please enclose a self-addressed stamped envelope for reply, or $1.00 to cover costs. If outside U.S.A., enclose international postal reply coupon.

Many of Llewellyn's authors have websites with additional information and resources.
For more information, please visit our website at
http://www.llewellyn.com

D.W. CROPPER

Bonechillers

13 TWISTED TALES OF TERROR

Llewellyn Publications
St. Paul, Minnesota

First Edition
First Printing, 2005

Art direction by Lynne Menturweck
Book design and layout by Donna Burch
Cover design by Ellen Dahl
Cover photograph © 2004, James Gritz/Photodisc
Editing by Rhiannon Ross
Interior flip art © 2005, jt yost illustration
Llewellyn is a registered trademark of Llewellyn Worldwide, Ltd.

Cover model(s) used for illustrative purposes only and may not endorse or
represent the book's subject.

Library of Congress Cataloging-in-Publication Data
Cropper, D. W. (David William), 1973-
  Bonechiller: 13 Twisted Tales of Terror/D.W. Cropper.
    p. cm.
    Contents: The Imaginary Friend-Snowbound-Running With the Pack-The Unfortunate Invitation-Devil From the Sky-Vengeance and Wrath-The Swith-Billy Don't Do It-Witch-Baby-The Parade of Night-Down, Down, Down-Orphan Asylum-In Shadows
    Summary: Thirteen stories of ghosts, vampires, witches, werewolves, and more.
ISBN: 0-7387-0758-9
    1. Horror tales, American. 2. Children's stories, America. [1. Horror stories. 2. Short stories.] 1. Title.
PZ7.C88213Bon2005
[Fic]--dc22

Llewellyn Worldwide does not participate in, endorse, or have any authority or responsibility concerning private business transactions between our authors and the public.

All mail addressed to the author is forwarded but the publisher cannot, unless specifically instructed by the author, give out an address or phone number.

Any Internet references contained in this work are current at publication time, but the publisher cannot guarantee that a specific location will continue to be maintained. Please refer to the publisher's website for links to authors' websites and other sources.

Llewellyn Publications
A Division of Llewellyn Worldwide, Ltd.
P.O. Box 64383, Dept. 0-7387-0758-9
St. Paul, MN 55164-0383, U.S.A.
www.llewellyn.com

Printed in the United States of America

Prepare to be terrified . . .

To my mother, Kathleen Ann Cropper,
a great reader who appreciated a
good, scary story as she appreciated all good stories.
Without her love and encouragement, I would never have had the
self-confidence to put pen to paper.

Contents

Contents

ONE

The Imaginary Friend

Sarah Kaufman's four-year-old brother spent most of his waking hours talking to someone named Bonnie—someone only he could see. Sarah's parents said it was just an imaginary friend. After all, a make-believe playmate seemed like a perfectly ordinary way of dealing with the family's recent move into the old house on Hudson Street. But Sarah was convinced there was something very strange about Bonnie.

She often stood listening on the staircase that led to little Henry's attic bedroom. Henry would sit Indian-style on the floor, with his head cocked up toward the rocking chair that had been left by the people from before. He'd murmur and pause, mutter and pause, as if listening for answers in between the things he had to say. And if Sarah stood very still and

listened very carefully, she swore she could hear the chair creak and begin to rock.

"Where would he come up with an old-fashioned name like 'Bonnie,' anyway?" Sarah asked her parents. "He barely knows the names of his own brothers and sisters."

"Don't be silly," her mother said.

"He might've picked the name up anywhere," her father insisted.

Sarah could see that she wasn't going to have any luck in convincing her parents there was something unusual about Henry's imaginary friend. Her older brothers and sisters weren't much help either. So she decided to question Henry on her own. She tried to draw him out of his shell, asking him all about Bonnie.

"Where does she come from? What does she look like? What do you talk about?"

She had to repeat the questions several times.

"She's from here," Henry finally said in response to her first question. "She was here when we came."

"Well, you must know more about her than that," Sarah scolded. "You talk all the time. Are you gonna tell me what you talk about?"

"No." Henry dipped his chin onto his chest. His hair was a mess of yellow curls.

"Why not?" Sarah persisted.

"Not suppose' to."

She wondered why he was being so secretive.

"Is Bonnie your age?" she asked.

"No," Henry answered, still not meeting his sister's gaze.

"Then how old is she?" Sarah demanded.

"Dunno," Henry grunted. "She's a lady."

Sarah gently placed her hands upon her brother's shoulders. "Please tell me what Bonnie looks like, Henry," she begged. "I'd really like to know. What color's her hair? What color are her eyes?"

"She doesn't have any eyes," Henry said, at last looking up and meeting his sister's gaze.

The hairs stood up on the back of Sarah's neck. "No eyes," she said. "That's kind of strange. How does Bonnie see?"

"Dunno," said Henry. "She just does."

"Well, then what's on her face . . . where her eyes should be?"

Henry shrugged. "Just two holes," he said. "All empty and black."

Sarah was mystified. Why would her brother imagine something so bizarre and consider it mundane? Either he was a very strange child, or there was something more to Bonnie than everyone else suspected.

The following morning Sarah woke in the wee hours before dawn. The house was dark and full of shadows. She sat upright in bed and listened.

Someone was singing.

The sound was so faint she could barely hear the words, but she recognized the melody.

Hush little ba-by don't say a word
Momma's gon-na buy you a mockingbird.
And if that mockin-bird don't sing
Momma's gonna buy you a diamond ring.

There was another sound, even fainter than the singing. Sarah felt certain it was the creaking of a rocking chair.

Sarah and Henry's mother never sang lullabies or, for that matter, any other variety of song, as she was entirely tone deaf. Yet this was distinctly a woman's voice.

Groggily, Sarah pulled herself out of bed and slipped down the hallway in her stocking feet. She followed the sound of the singing and soon found herself standing at the foot of the stairwell that led up to her brother's bedroom. The singing continued. It was still faint—little more than a whisper—but now Sarah could hear the words quite clearly.

And if that mockingbird don't sing
Momma's gonna buy you a diamond ring.
And if that diamond ring don't shine
It'll surely break this heart of mine.

Sarah began climbing the steps one at a time. She was fully awake now, and her legs were shaking quite badly. Her whole body seemed filled with icy water, yet she had to see.

Eventually she reached the landing, where the creaking of the floorboards betrayed her, and the singing abruptly ended. She froze in place and peered into the darkened room.

A shaft of pale light slanted down from the window and shone on her brother's sleeping form. At first this was all she could see, but then her eyes began to adjust to the darkness. She detected movement and heard the steady squeak of the rocking chair. But when she took a step forward, she saw that the chair was empty. She stared at it, hypnotized, and slowly realized the rocking motion was dying down. It was as if someone had jumped up out of the chair only a moment before.

"W-who's there?" Sarah called, her voice breaking terribly.

No one answered.

Then something unseen shoved her back out onto the landing, where she hit the floorboards with a thud and very nearly tumbled down the stairs.

"Leave us alone!" hissed an unfamiliar, female voice.

That's when Sarah caught the most fleeting glimpse of a woman standing in the center of Henry's bedroom. A woman dressed in

a very old-fashioned dress with ghastly gray skin and a tangled mess of snaky black hair. But worst of all was the woman's face: there were no eyes, but only two round voids, as empty and black as Henry had described.

Then with a great gust of wind Henry's bedroom door was slammed shut.

Sarah sat on the landing in shock, her heartbeat racing and the slamming sound reverberating in her ears. As soon as she recovered, she leapt back to her feet and began pounding on the door. Frantically, she tried the handle, but it wouldn't turn.

"Let me in, Henry!" she cried. "Let me in!"

Soon her mother and father came to see what all the noise was about. They stumbled up the stairs in their rumpled bedclothes. Sarah's other brothers and sisters trailed along behind.

"Whatever's the matter?" her mother asked.

"I saw her! I saw her!" Sarah shouted, still pounding on the door. "She's in there with him."

"Who's in there?" her father asked.

"It's Bonnie," Sarah told her parents. "She's real!"

"Nonsense," her mother said.

Her father tried the door. "It's locked," he reported.

Mrs. Kaufman stepped forward and gently knocked. "Henry, dear, it's Mommy. Please open the door and let us in."

A few moments later they heard someone fumbling with the lock, and the door swung open to reveal Henry standing in his pajamas. He looked up at them and rubbed his sleepy eyes with his fist.

A thorough search of the room was enough to convince Sarah's mother and father that she'd been imagining things.

"There's simply no one here," her father said. "Not a soul."

"I know what I saw," Sarah insisted. "*And* what I felt."

"We'll talk about it later," her mother said. "Right now I think we should all get back to bed. It's still too early for breakfast."

Reluctantly, Sarah agreed to return to her own bedroom. It was pointless to argue with her parents once their minds were made up. Besides, whatever Bonnie was or whatever her intentions were, it seemed that she had no immediate plans to harm Henry.

Mrs. Kaufman began tucking Henry back into bed.

"And as for you, young man," she told him. "I don't want you to ever lock your door again. That upsets Mommy very much."

"That's okay," Henry said, staring listlessly up at her.

"What do you mean 'that's okay,'" his mother demanded. "What's okay?"

7

"I mean it's okay if you're mad," Henry explained in a rather matter-of-fact tone. "It doesn't matter, 'cause Bonnie says you won't be my mommy for much longer."

From that morning on, Mrs. Kaufman became very upset whenever Henry mentioned Bonnie. In fact, she forbade Henry to talk to his "imaginary" friend ever again.

But Sarah knew that her brother's conversations with Bonnie hadn't ended. His voice only became more hushed, as he whispered into the darkest hours of the night. One morning she confronted him, once again placing her hands on his shoulders, as it was the only way to get his attention.

"I thought Mom told you not to talk to Bonnie anymore?" she asked.

"It doesn't matter," Henry replied with a shrug. "Bonnie says I'll soon be with her for good."

"What does that mean?" Sarah demanded, gently shaking him.

But Henry would say no more.

Sarah became determined to find out just who or what Bonnie was, yet her brother flat-out refused to answer any more questions. She knew, however, that Henry'd only begun talking to Bonnie after the family's move to the house on Hudson Street. So she decided to research the history of the house.

She went to the library and shifted through all of the old newspapers, hoping to find some clue in regard to the identity of her brother's very real "imaginary" friend. It took hours, but her efforts paid off at last.

She found an article from the 1860s about a woman named Bonnie O'Rourke. Bonnie lived her entire life in the house on Hudson Street. According to the article she'd been a young mother and wife, whose husband was killed in the Civil War. This left Bonnie to care for her little boy, who was just a toddler, all by herself.

Unfortunately, the local authorities soon decided that Bonnie and her little boy couldn't get by without her husband to provide for them. They wanted her to take the boy and live with relatives in San Francisco. But Bonnie refused to leave the house on Hudson Street. She said it was the only home they'd ever known.

Because of her stubbornness, the locals decided she wasn't fit to raise her son on her own—they figured she must've gone mad over the loss of her husband. So one day they came to the house and took the boy away.

Bonnie was devastated. Her son was all she'd had left. If she hadn't been slipping into madness before they took him, she certainly lost her sanity after he was gone. According

to the neighbors, she couldn't stand seeing all of the things that reminded her of the boy, yet couldn't bear to leave the house either. So she took a course of action that would seem reasonable only to a woman who'd gone completely insane: she gouged her own eyes out.

A few months later Bonnie plummeted to her death from the window of the attic room where Sarah's little brother now slept. Whether it was suicide or an accident, no one knew.

As soon as she'd finished reading, Sarah hurried out of the library and ran home as fast as her legs could carry her. She now knew that Bonnie was the ghost of a woman who'd had her only son, a boy Henry's very age, torn from her arms. Suddenly Henry's comment about being with Bonnie "for good soon" took on an even more sinister meaning.

Sarah was frantic to get home.

When she reached Hudson Street she looked up and caught a glimpse of Henry peering down from his bedroom window. She put her head down and ran even harder, and by the time she reached the front lawn she was panting for breath. She looked up again and saw that Henry had opened his window, and was now pushing against the screen with both hands. Sarah wanted to scream, but found she could only wheeze and pant.

She burst through the front door and scrambled up the stairs, taking them two at a time. By the time she reached the landing Henry had succeeded in pushing the screen out and was climbing onto the windowsill. Now Sarah did manage to scream, and her bloodcurdling cry of desperation pierced the silence of the otherwise peaceful neighborhood. She bounded across the small bedroom in three long strides and grabbed for Henry's arm just as he began to slip from the windowsill.

But she grasped only air.

Henry was a few feet beneath the window ledge and slipping down the steep slope of the roof, knocking the shingles loose as he went. The concrete walkway loomed some thirty-five feet below. Sarah stretched herself as far out of the window as possible and made another grab.

The very tips of her fingers slid underneath the collar of her brother's shirt and, just barely, she was able to keep a hold of him.

"Leggo! Leggo!" he yelled. "I wanna be with Bonnie!"

Gradually Sarah began to pull him back through the window. Soon her mother appeared at her shoulder.

"What on earth is going on here?" Mrs. Kaufman cried, helping her daughter yank Henry the rest of the way into the bedroom.

"I wanna be with Bonnie!" Henry yelled again. "She said if I just took two little steps out my window I'd be with her forever 'n ever."

Mrs. Kaufman was so shaken she couldn't even speak.

Sarah pulled the window shut, a great sense of relief washing over her. Now there was no way her mother could deny that Bonnie was a very real and very scary presence.

Almost immediately the family decided to move out of the house on Hudson Street. And while the arrangements for the move were being made, everyone kept a close eye on Henry. He was never allowed to be alone—he even slept with his mother and father.

Sarah felt as though she could relax for the first time in weeks. She didn't hear any more whispering or singing and she was actually able to sleep at night.

In just a few days a new house was located, a moving truck was rented, and all of the family's belongings were packed. And on the last night the family was to spend in the old house, Sarah fell into the deepest sleep she'd enjoyed in a long time. Little Henry was downstairs, safe and snug and in bed with his mother and father.

Or so everyone thought.

It wasn't singing or whispering that woke Sarah this time. It was the smell of smoke. She woke up choking and could barely breathe. The smoke was drifting into her room in thick clouds that seemed to be rolling down from Henry's old bedroom. Then she heard Henry's voice and knew that

he'd somehow snuck up into the attic room. She wanted to yell "fire," but her throat had filled up with the smoke and she could hardly make a sound.

The crackling of the flames soon became audible and the smoke grew ever thicker. Yet Henry prattled on and on, as if he and Bonnie were enjoying a perfectly pleasant evening together.

Although it took every ounce of strength she possessed, Sarah started to climb out of bed. She'd just managed to pull herself to her feet when she heard Henry call out to Bonnie.

"Bonnie, Bonnie!" he cried. "Where are you going? Don't leave me by myself!"

Then Sarah heard the sound of footsteps bounding down the attic stairs. And the next thing she knew she was knocked back onto her bed, with a pair of icy cold hands wrapped around her neck.

"I told you to leave us alone!" hissed the angry voice.

Sarah clawed at her throat, desperately trying to peel off the invisible fingers. But Bonnie was too strong. Sarah began to fear that she'd get the life choked out of her.

"He's mine!" Bonnie hissed. "He's mine!"

And suddenly Sarah saw the horrible face, with its snaky hair and empty, rotting eye-sockets. Bonnie loomed above her, the icy hands tightening.

Sarah knew she had to do something if she was going to survive. So, in her extreme desperation, she reached up and shoved her thumbs into the cavernous eye-sockets. She didn't think a dead person could feel pain, but if it was possible to shock a ghost this certainly did the trick. Bonnie released her chokehold and flew backward, covering her face in her hands and wailing. Either she was surprised at Sarah's boldness or she was ashamed at the sudden reminder of her grotesque deformity.

Sarah seized the opportunity and sprang out of the room. She darted up the stairs and into the attic. Henry was sitting Indian-style next to the rocking chair and crying. She grabbed him by the arm and yanked him off the floor. Then they tumbled back down the stairs, the house becoming an inferno around them. Great, flaming chunks of wood rained down from the ceiling, and the staircase seemed on the verge of collapse.

Sarah heard her parents calling for them and fought her way through the smoke. The next thing she knew her father was carrying her out onto the front lawn. Henry was still crying, but now he was safely cradled in his mother's arms.

The fire trucks arrived shortly, their sirens blaring, but it was too late. The fire had spread rapidly, and now it engulfed the entire house.

Eventually the firemen would decide that the blaze had begun in Henry's attic bedroom—another unfortunate case

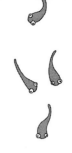

of a child playing with matches. But Sarah knew there was more to the story. She imagined Bonnie stealthily luring Henry out of the safety of his mother and father's bedroom and all but placing the matches in his hand.

Of course none of that mattered now, as the entire family stood by and watched the old house on Hudson Street burn all the way to the ground. And over the crackling of the fire and the crumbling of the walls, they soon heard another sound. This sound was so faint they could barely make it out, but it was almost certainly the sound of a woman singing. Sarah recognized the melody and knew what was being sung.

And if that mockingbird don't sing
Momma's gonna buy you a diamond ring.
And if that diamond ring don't shine
It'll surely break this heart of mine.

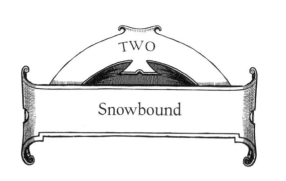

TWO

Snowbound

Over a hundred years ago a railroad was winding its way across the country. Men were laying tracks through the towns, the cities, and across the Great Plains.

Wing Lee worked on a railroad gang way out West. In that part of the country the mountains rose up into the clouds and stretched the length of the horizon. The railroad couldn't go around these huge obstacles, so Wing and the other men had the job of digging tunnels straight through tons and tons of dirt and rock. They bored in with picks and shovels, and when they hit the solid rock, they blasted it to bits with TNT.

Wing was only seventeen, but he was already an experienced hammer swinger. He drove steel spikes into the face of the mountain,

then went ducking for cover as the spikes were removed and the holes plugged up with dynamite.

Wing didn't really mind the earth-shaking explosion that followed, but he hated the awful shower of dirt and rocks. He sometimes feared it would never end and he'd be buried in that mountain, half a world away from the Cantonese village where he was born.

By November it was already snowing. All of the other crews gave up and left for the winter, but Wing and the rest of the Chinese men stayed behind. They had no place else to go—their homes were in China—so they kept on tunneling.

The heavy snow fell in the mountains. It piled up at the mouth of the tunnel and threatened to drown out the daylight. Late one afternoon, Wing and his best friend Chang stood watching as the thick powder piled ever higher. It was like a great white wave about to wash over them.

"We'll be trapped," Chang said. "This tunnel will be our tomb."

"Don't worry," Wing told him. "We have plenty of supplies and there's enough air. We can survive in the tunnel until spring."

"No," Chang insisted. "They'll get us before then."

Wing laughed. "Who'll get us?" he asked.

But Chang wouldn't say. He only stared at the rising snowdrift the way a condemned man might stare at the gallows.

Wing knew the mountains were full of myths and legend—trolls and ghosts and evil jinn. He liked some of the stories, but he knew they were just make-believe. They were silly tales and superstitions. Even his favorite story—the one about a hammer swinger who lost his life in a contest with a steam shovel—couldn't possibly be true. No man, no matter how strong, could ever keep pace with a steam shovel. Some of the stories were quite scary, however, and Wing suspected that Chang had spent too much time listening to the old men who liked to spin such yarns.

That night the snow completely swallowed the mouth of the tunnel. In the morning there was only the light from the torches.

As the mountain froze, it became harder to dig. Each swing of his hammer caused crippling pains to shoot like electricity through Wing's bones. The other men were suffering just as much, especially the older fellows.

Eventually the men had to stop work altogether. They huddled around small fires deep in the mountain and began the long winter's wait. Some men regretted their decision to stay and spoke of burrowing through the snow at the mouth of the tunnel.

The old men chided them not to be ridiculous. The snow was too deep. If they tried to dig their way to freedom they would either freeze or suffocate. Besides, even if

19

they did manage to dig their way out, where would they go? The nearest settlement was all the way at the bottom of the mountain.

But Wing's friend Chang became even more desperate to escape the tunnel. He kept babbling on about how "they" were going to get him. And whenever Wing pressed him to explain exactly what he meant, Chang would grow suddenly quiet. Then he'd watch Wing very closely, as if he suspected his friend might turn out to be one of them—whoever they were—after all.

One night Wing woke from a bad dream and noticed that his friend was missing. Chang had been in a bad state of mind, and Wing worried that he might injure himself in the darkened tunnel. He set out at once to conduct a search.

After stumbling around for several minutes he noticed a lone figure standing way up at the head of the tunnel. It was Chang. His thin frame was silhouetted against the expanse of ice and snow that had trapped the railroad men.

"Chang?" Wing called, approaching cautiously. "What are you doing?"

Chang didn't answer. He was staring up at the icy mass as if he were about to try and dig his way out with his bare hands.

"Come on, Chang," Wing said. "It's too cold out here. You should come back and sit by the fire."

"No," Chang said. "They will get us. I have to stay alert."

Wing knew his friend hadn't slept for several days. "Look," he told him. "If you come back with me, I'll sit up

with you, and we can watch for them together."

Chang turned around and faced him. He
seemed a little calmer now, and looked as
though he really did want to go and sit by the
fire. "And you promise not to let them get
me?" he asked hopefully.

"That's right," Wing told him. "They're
not going to get you. There's nothing to be
afraid of. They don't exist."

Just as Wing was reassuring his friend,
however, seven heads emerged from the
snow and rose on impossibly long necks all
the way to the ceiling of the tunnel. The
seven faces had a human-like quality to them,
but they weren't quite human. They were as
white as fish bellies and had small eyes and
very large mouths. They peered down on
poor Chang, their long necks writhing and
undulating like snakes. Chang didn't see these
awful necks and heads, as he had his back
turned to them.

Wing wanted to warn him. He'd just
promised not to let them get Chang. But
then he hadn't really believed that they existed. Now here they were and he found himself paralyzed.

In an instant the seven heads struck. The wide mouths opened to reveal row upon row of steely teeth. The long necks wrapped around Chang's legs and arms. The faces turned gleeful as they bit into his shoulders and neck. Chang screamed like a wild animal in its death throes.

"NO!" Wing cried, rushing forward to free his friend.

It was too late. The necks and heads pulled Chang back and into the snow. And within seconds both Wing's best friend and the strange monsters that had attacked him were gone.

Wing ran back down the tunnel and roused the others.

"It's Chang," he cried. "Poor Chang! They've got him!"

The men grabbed their picks and shovels and lit the torches. They proceeded up to the mouth of the tunnel, with Wing leading the way.

But when the armed party arrived at the dreaded spot, they found nothing. There was no sign that Chang or the monsters had even existed, save for the horrible images seared in Wing's brain.

"It was here, I tell you," Wing said. "They took him and disappeared into the snow drift."

"Well, there's nothing here now," the men said. "Maybe you imagined it."

"Then where is Chang?" he demanded.

"That man has been nothing but trouble," the others said. "He's probably gotten lost somewhere in the tunnel."

"No!" Wing insisted. "I saw them get him. They were horrible."

"But there's nothing here. You imagined it. They don't exist."

And as if these were the magic words, the heads began to emerge from the snow. The long necks rose high into the air, as the white faces gazed down on the terrified men. Then a large torpedo-shaped body burst into the tunnel, and Wing saw that all seven of the necks radiated from it like the branches of a tree.

The thing was like a giant squid, with terrible heads at the ends of its tentacles. Wing had never seen or even imagined anything like it. The monster had a million tiny legs, like those of a millipede, with which it scurried up the walls and ceiling of the tunnel.

Suddenly there were seven more heads poking out of the snow and peering at the men. Then another seven. And another seven. The torpedo-shaped monsters—each about fifteen feet long—oozed out of the snow one by one.

The railroad men stared in disbelief, as the things came at them, hissing and showing their sharp teeth. Every man ran for his life.

Wing tried to rally his countrymen. He told them there was nowhere to run and they

must stand and fight. But no one listened to him until it was already too late for several men.

The monsters began to snatch up the unlucky and the slow. They plucked men off the floor of the tunnel, wrapping them in their necks, the vicious heads chewing and rending the flesh of their victims. At least half a dozen railroad men were killed.

Finally, Wing managed to gather the survivors in a circle, and they made a stand. The monsters came at them, four long bodies and twenty-eight horrible heads. The heads kept striking, trying to pick them off one at a time. But Wing kept his friends banded together, and they swung their picks and shovels feverishly.

A few more men were snatched up and pulled screaming to their deaths. However, the others soon learned that the monsters weren't invincible. A few of the terrible heads were lopped off and went rolling along the ground.

One severed head rolled right up next to a man's leg and bit him on the shin. The poor fellow shrieked and tried desperately to pull the vise-like jaws open. Wing saw what had happened and fought his way over to the man. He hefted his hammer high and brought it down, smashing the head like a ripe melon. It opened its vicious mouth, and squealed like a piglet, as the blow reduced it to a puddle of squishy slime.

Slowly the men managed to drive the squid-like monsters back to mouth of the tunnel. Then the horrid things retreated, slipping back into the snowdrift as easily as eels slip under the sea.

The railroad men cheered. They had survived—at least for the moment. Wing was glad to be alive, yet he had a feeling the monsters would be back.

They built up the campfires, determined to stay vigilant. Men were posted as sentries, while the others tried to sleep, but it was difficult.

The old men were consulted as to what the monsters might be. "They remind me of a legend I heard once a long time ago," one wizened fellow said. "Seven headed creatures called Chum-Chum that swim through the snow the way fish swim in the sea."

"Yes, I've heard of such creatures," another man said. "They sleep in caves in the summer. Then in the winter they come out to feed."

Wing thought of poor Chang. His friend had always been fascinated by such stories. And he had always believed they were true. Now Wing knew he'd been right. Chang tried to warn him. He tried to warn them all, but no one had listened. Now Chang was gone forever, and they might all suffer the same fate. Something drastic had to be done. But what?

Suddenly, Wing remembered the TNT. It was stored in crates deep in the tunnel. He told the others, but they thought it was too dangerous. The dynamite was very unstable and, if they tried to use it against the Chum-Chum, they might very well cause a cave-in and bury themselves alive.

Wing was about to argue that they had no other choice, but he never got the chance. The next wave of Chum-Chum burst into the tunnel and began scurrying toward the campfires. The monsters had multiplied again and a score of menacing heads bobbed and wove their way down the tunnel. In fact, there were so many Chum-Chum, some of them crawled along the ceiling, their maniacal faces hanging upside down.

The railroad men grabbed their tools and torches and defended themselves the best they could. Wing grabbed his hammer and swung like mad, all the while holding a torch clenched between his teeth. But the monsters were simply too numerous. Men were snatched up left and right. They flailed and screamed, but it was hopeless. Once a Chum-Chum had a man wrapped in its strangling necks, the heads soon made short work of him.

The survivors were driven deeper into the tunnel, where Wing discovered that he was one of the last men standing. He found himself cornered by three monsters. The largest one came at him, all seven of its heads hissing and snapping.

Wing raised his hammer. He was ready to defend himself to the last. But just as he thought the monster would strike it paused and stared at him with all fourteen of its eyes. Then all seven of the heads spoke as one, their voices echoing off the walls. "You cannot escape us," they hissed. "This mountain is our home. Stop fighting us and your death will be quick and only a little painful."

And as they spoke these last words the seven faces began grinding and gnashing their terrible teeth.

Wing was determined not to surrender. He bellowed a fierce war cry and fought like a man possessed. He swung his hammer like that legendary hero who'd died after defeating the steam shovel. He struck one of the Chum-Chum's heads and it spun like a tetherball, wrapping around the neck of the head nearest it.

The monster drew back. Wing swung again and again, gradually fighting his way out of the corner. But it was only a temporary victory. The monsters just kept coming. They pressed ever deeper into the tunnel, and Wing had no choice but to retreat.

He inched backward, defending himself all the way. Then he stumbled over a large crate and fell on his back. Several monsters had him hemmed in now, and he knew that he was completely alone. Every other man had been dragged to his death—screaming.

The white faces rose up all around him. Wing closed his eyes, waiting for them to strike. Then he realized what it was he'd just tripped over: a crate filled with TNT. The Chum-Chum had chased him all the way to the very back of the tunnel where the dynamite was kept.

Wing leapt to his feet and swung his hammer in a great arc. The Chum-Chum reared back their heads. Then they all began whispering to him to give up the fight.

Wing ignored them and smashed open the crate. The torch was still gripped between his teeth. He knew he had only to light the fuse of a single stick of TNT. That would start a chain reaction of explosions and collapse the entire tunnel.

"What are you doing, little man?" the Chum-Chum taunted. "You can't escape us now."

"Maybe not," Wing said. "But I can take some of you wretched devils with me."

At that he pulled out a stick of the dynamite, touched the torch to its fuse, and dropped it back in the crate.

The heads came down like the tendrils of a man-eating plant. Wing jumped and rolled out of the way. Several of the heads butted one another, and some of the necks became entangled.

Wing got to his feet and as ran fast as he could, swinging his hammer every which way. He jumped over necks and dodged striking heads. He thought he saw a bit of sunlight peeking through the snow at the mouth of the tunnel. Then he was bit on the ankle and pulled into the air. He kicked and struggled, but the Chum-Chum had him. He became ensnared in the monster's necks, and the seven faces smiled at him.

All seven smiles soon faded, however, when the explosions rocked the entire mountain. There were deafening screams as the monsters in the rear of the tunnel were blown into thousands of bits. Slimy chunks of Chum-Chum were plastered all over the walls, and hundreds of small heads rolled along the ground in a smothering cloud of smoke. Then there was a great rumbling and the entire tunnel began to collapse.

Wing found himself on the ground. The monster had dropped him in the confusion. He crawled toward the daylight, but the smoke swallowed everything. He began to choke, and realized he was being buried alive.

He put his head down, resigned to his fate at last. But just as he was starting to black out, he felt himself being dragged toward the mouth of the tunnel.

The next thing Wing knew, he was outside lying in the sunshine. Someone stood above him. It wasn't a Chum-Chum, but a man. He was a big fellow, broad-shouldered and full of muscles. Wing couldn't see clearly,

as his vision was blurry, but he made out that the man was black and bald.

"You're gonna be all right, Mister," the man said in a booming voice. Then he heaved Wing up on his shoulders and carried him away from the collapsed tunnel.

Wing fell into a deep sleep. When he woke up he found he was lying alone at the very bottom of the mountain. He pulled himself to his feet and looked about. There was no sign of the man who had saved him.

He stumbled through the snow for hours before he finally saw the faint light of a distant town. He pressed on and reached civilization at last. The townspeople eyed him suspiciously, but an innkeeper saw that Wing was half dead and took pity on him. The kind fellow sheltered him in the inn, fed him, and gave him hot tea.

Slowly Wing was revived and he began to tell the innkeeper his incredible story. He told of the snowstorm and the monstrous Chum-Chum, and he was stunned when the old man seemed to believe the bizarre tale. In fact, the man nodded gravely and said he'd heard stories of such creatures before.

So Wing went on and told of how the black man had rescued him. At this, the innkeeper did act surprised and seemed more than a little doubtful. He asked Wing to describe the man in more detail. Wing recounted all that he could recall.

"It's just not possible," the innkeeper said. "The man you describe couldn't have rescued you. You must have hallucinated."

"What do you mean?" Wing asked. He didn't understand why the old fellow believed the incredible story about the Chum-Chum and not the simple story of his rescue. "Why couldn't I have been rescued by such a man? He was there, I tell you."

The innkeeper only shook his head. "No, my friend. You are mistaken. The man you describe died a long time ago. He was a hammer swinger named John Henry and he died in a contest with a steam shovel. He beat the machine, but lost his life. They buried him on the mountain many years before you were born."

Wing stared into the fire and thought of all the myths and legends and silly stories the old railroad men used to tell. He thought of the trolls and ghosts and jinn. Now he knew what Chang had known all along. Not all of them were simply stories. And some of them weren't so silly after all.

31

THREE

Running with the Pack

Frank Palgrave's grandfather had always been there for him. Ever since his father died when Frank was just a baby, he and his mother had lived with the kind, old fellow. Now Gramps was sixty-four, but he was still healthy and strong. He had big brown eyes, which were gentle and sad like those of a basset hound. More than anything else, Frank wanted to be like his grandfather.

He even wanted to join the secret society of which Gramps was a member.

They called themselves the Pack, and met once every month down in the basement. Frank had been dying to know what went on in these meetings his entire life.

The basement was the only part of the house that he and his mother were forbidden to enter. Many a night he lay awake, trying to

imagine what was unfolding in that dark place underneath the house. Yet no matter how long he listened, he never heard a sound from below.

Then one night he happened to be looking out his window, hypnotized by the ghostly pallor of the moon and the icy twinkling of the stars, when he sensed movement in the yard below. He glanced down just in time to see several dark shapes emerging from the cellar. They scrambled across the lawn in single file and disappeared into the woods. They had to be Gramps and the other members of the Pack, but Frank had no clue what they were doing running into the woods in the middle of the night.

At school the next morning he told his two best friends, Sally and John Barrow, what he'd seen.

"What do you suppose they were doing out there?" Sally wondered.

"I don't know," Frank said. "But I'm sure gonna try'n find out."

"Maybe they were trying to solve the murders," John offered.

It was true that Halloway County had the highest murder rate in the state. Over the years several people had been killed in gruesome fashion in their own homes. The police had no clue as to whom or what was responsible.

"Why don't you just go on and ask your grandfather if you can join his weird club?" John asked, as the bell rang and everyone began milling toward class. "I mean, if you're so curious about what they do, wouldn't joining 'em be a good way to find out?"

"I don't know," Sally said. "With all due respect to your grandfather and all, that club sounds pretty creepy. Like, what's with the sneaking around in the woods at night?"

"Ah, they were probably communing with nature or something," John said. "I bet they usually just hang out in the basement and drink beer."

Frank said goodbye to his friends and hurried to class. He knew that what John had said made a lot of sense. For months he'd been trying to work up the nerve to ask his grandfather if he could join the Pack. But the timing never seemed quite right.

As usual, it wasn't long before Frank got into trouble. His teacher caught him sketching in his notebook and completely ignoring the morning's lesson. She sent him straight to the principal's office.

Frank was no stranger to Principal Stempel's office. He hated the stale smell of old papers and the mean stare of the secretary. But most of all he hated breathing in the utter stench of Stempel's awful cologne. The thick musty smell constantly swirled about the man and always made Frank feel sick.

"More artwork, Mr. Palgrave?" Stempel asked. He sat behind his desk, examining the sketch. His beady eyes were narrowed behind his glasses and his thin lips were twisted into a sneer. The smell of the cologne was so noxious Frank had to hold his breath.

"I've warned you before," Stempel said. "Now you've earned yourself a week of detention."

Frank was about to protest—it seemed so unfair to get a whole week of detention over one lousy drawing—but Stempel held up his hand for silence.

"And not only are you going to spend a week in detention," he continued, turning the notebook around and waving Frank's own sketch at him. "I think we'll show this drawing to your grandfather as well. That way he can see just what it is his grandson does all day."

Frank's eyes widened in surprise. It was bad enough that Stempel was going to tell Gramps he'd been goofing off in class. But the fact that Gramps was going to be shown that particular drawing could prove catastrophic.

Frank had been in a daze and hadn't even realized what it was he'd sketched. And now that Stempel held the notebook out, he was horrified to see an eerie depiction of the dark shapes emerging from the cellar beneath his bedroom window.

As soon as he got home from school Gramps called him into the study. Frank felt so angry with Stempel he could barely see straight. He slinked into the room, his head hung low. Gramps was sitting behind his desk, holding the sketch in front of him.

"Your principal gave me this drawing," he said, staring at Frank with his sad eyes. "Is there something you want to tell me about it?"

"I wasn't spying," Frank blurted out. "I just happened to be looking out my window last night."

"At two o'clock in the morning?"

"I couldn't sleep, I guess."

Gramps leaned back in his chair and folded his big hairy hands. "You've always been curious about the Pack. Haven't you, Frank?"

Frank was stunned. This was the first time his grandfather ever made a direct reference to the secret society. Frank's mother often warned him the subject was strictly taboo and should never be spoken of. But now that Gramps finally seemed willing to talk about it, he figured he was free to speak his mind.

"Yes, sir," he said. "I've wanted to know what you guys do down there ever since I was a little kid. That's why I did that drawing. Stempel had no right to take it. I hate that guy, Gramps. He's always on my back. I hate his guts!"

Frank realized he was rambling and his words trailed off. His grandfather was smiling at him, with a peculiar expression on his face. He held his breath and awaited the sentencing.

"Well," Gramps began at last, "It sounds as though this *Stempel* has already punished you enough."

Gramps was always respectful toward authority figures, yet he said Stempel's name with contempt, as if it was all he could do to keep himself from spitting on the floor at the mention of someone so repugnant.

"Why don't you just go on up to your room and do your homework," Gramps finished. "And we won't mention any of this to your mother."

"Okay, Gramps," Frank agreed. "Whatever you say."

Somewhat confused, he hurried out of the study and up to his room. Normally his grandfather was very strict when it came to misbehavior, and this sudden turnaround made Frank feel strange. It had seemed like Gramps was about to ask him to actually join the Pack. But he hadn't.

Frank was relieved not to be punished, yet he couldn't help feeling disappointed. Gramps didn't want him to be a member of the Pack. That was all there was to it. Maybe his grandfather just didn't want Frank around so much.

During the course of the next few weeks, nothing else out of the ordinary happened. Frank fell back into his normal routine. The Pack seemed as mysterious as ever, and he felt there was no possibility Gramps would ever ask him to join.

But then one day after school, he went up to his room to find a long black robe hanging from his closet door. Inside the pocket of the robe was a piece of paper, rolled up like a scroll. Frank stretched it out and saw that it was an invitation.

You have been selected as an initiate of the Pack. Come to the meeting room at midnight. Discuss this summons with no one, or face the penalty of death.

The brief note was signed only with a symbol, which was a strange five-pointed star.

At midnight the kitchen was deserted and darkened. The only light came from the full moon, which shone through the window over the stove. Yet the door leading to the basement stood ajar. As far back as Frank could remember this door had always been closed and locked. He approached the door and saw a stone staircase that wound down into the vast darkness. Suddenly something his mother often said sprang to mind: *Be careful what you wish for, Frank. You might just get it.* He took a deep breath and slowly descended the stairs. The basement seemed cavernous,

the steps going deeper and deeper. *No wonder why I could never hear anything*, Frank thought.

Far above him, the door creaked shut and someone locked the bolt. But Frank kept moving down. At last he rounded a corner and saw a lighted doorway. Inside, in a room with stone walls and a stone floor, several robed figures sat around a star-shaped table. One of the figures looked up as Frank approached—it was his grandfather.

"Please join us, Frank," Gramps said, indicating the empty chair next to him.

Frank sat down and glanced around the table. He recognized most of the men right away. They were just average guys, who went to work in the morning and came home at night—of course some nights were exceptions to the rule. Several of them were drinking beer out of large steins, and Frank wondered if John wasn't right about the Pack being an excuse for Gramps and his friends to hang out in the basement and drink beer.

"I hereby call this meeting to order," Gramps said, banging a gavel, which appeared to have been made from the horn of some large animal.

"You all know my grandson," Gramps continued. "He's a good boy who's becoming a man. And ever since we lost his father, Frank's been like a son to me. That's why it gives me great pride to move that he be initiated into the Pack."

Gramps was beaming at him, and Frank could feel his own chest swelling with pride. All the members of the Pack were smiling at him and nodding their heads.

"I second the motion," said a man with red hair.

His grandfather stood up and placed his large hand on Frank's shoulder. He was still smiling, but there was something different about his eyes—something strange. "All those in favor of the motion, say 'aye'," he called.

The "ayes" erupted all around the table.

"Frank Palgrave," Gramps declared. "From this day onward you will be changed. You will be powerful, unstoppable—a part of something far greater than yourself."

Gramps' voice became guttural—almost a growl in fact—and there was something very odd about his face. The features seemed to be stretching out—especially the nose and mouth—and coarse gray hairs were springing up everywhere.

Frank looked around frantically and saw that all of the men were changing. Some of them jumped up on their chairs, or even on the table, growling and sprouting dark hair. Then their bodies began to contort, their arms lengthening and their hands morphing into giant claws. They were ugly and twisted, with great hunched backs—a horrendous cross between animals and men.

Oh, this is just great, Frank thought, *werewolves!*

He was paralyzed with fear. And, with lightening quickness, the creature that his grandfather had turned into sank its razor sharp fangs into his shoulder. Frank cried out in pain, staring helplessly at the big grizzly muzzle that was wrapped around his shoulder. The creature released him and reared back, letting out a prodigious howl. Frank clutched his wound, but the blood was already running down his arm.

All of the other werewolves began howling as well, and soon the entire basement resounded with the bloodcurdling cries.

"Feel the power surging through you, boy," said the monster that only moments before had been Frank's grandfather. "Let it make you strong."

The voice was horribly distorted, little more than a growl, but it was definitely his grandfather's voice. Despite what the monster said, however, Frank didn't feel powerful. He only felt sick, like he'd been poisoned. He collapsed on the floor and writhed in agony.

"Rise, rise!" chanted the monster. "Rise and feel the change come over you."

Frank began to feel differently. He got a strange tingling sensation and it seemed as though something was welling up inside him. He felt a great hunger, yearning to be sated. Then he could feel the change coming over him. It was like his body was about to turn itself inside out. He wanted to resist the transformation, but the hunger was too strong. He simply couldn't control it.

He could feel the bristly fur sprouting from beneath his skin. He could feel his body changing, as the bones of his skeleton re-arranged themselves. He could taste the razor sharp teeth forming in his mouth. And he could see the razor sharp claws shooting from his fingertips.

The next thing he knew he was up on the table, his long rangy body coiled like a spring. He felt every bit as powerful as Gramps had promised, and he was consumed with the re-lentless hunger. He reared back and let out an earsplitting howl.

Soon the entire Pack was bursting from the cellar and into the night. Frank—or at least the beast that had been Frank—ran right alongside them, barely aware of who he was or what he was doing. The werewolves bounded into the woods, splashing through mud puddles and scattering the other animals. Their yellow eyes cut far into the darkness and their long limbs sent them vaulting over logs and underbrush.

The Pack picked up a scent and followed the odor back out of the woods. Their newest member was particularly familiar with the thick musty smell. And, although he

couldn't remember where he'd smelled it before, he knew it'd often made him feel sick.

But he didn't feel sick now, as he crept out of the woods and across someone's backyard. He was only hungry, insatiably hungry.

There were no lights on in the strange house—it was far too late. The other members of the Pack hung back, while the old grizzled one waited for him near the back door. He moved forward, crawling on all fours through the long grass.

"It's time to complete your initiation," the old one snarled. "Lead the Pack into that house and do as your instincts tell you!"

He found he couldn't speak, but he responded with a low growl. Then he rose up on two legs and smashed through the back door, his thick claws easily splintering the wood and sending shards in all directions. He stormed up the stairs, the musty smell filling his nostrils and leading him straight to the man.

The man had short dark hair and a thin mouth. He'd just managed to put his glasses on and now he was sitting up in bed and holding his hands in front of his face. "No!" he screamed. "Stay away! Stay away!"

The creature pounced, its fellows filing into the room behind it. And then the entire world was awash in red.

Frank woke late the next morning. He remembered very little—only the awful hunger and the sea of red. But now he was in his bedroom, staring up at the ceiling, and none of it seemed real. Yet he knew it was. He could feel it in his heart. He'd killed an innocent man.

He was late for school. He threw some clothes on and rushed out without eating breakfast (but then he wasn't exactly hungry anymore).

When he got to school it didn't seem to matter that he was late. No one noticed. The whole school was in an uproar about something. People were wandering around the halls jabbering on and on about a terrible tragedy. Some people were even crying.

He ran into Sally and asked her what was going on.

"You mean you haven't heard yet?" she asked.

"I just got here," he explained.

"It's awful, Frank," she said. "Someone murdered Principal Stempel last night!"

Suddenly Frank recalled the thick, musty smell of the man's cologne. And he felt sick— sick in his body and sick in his soul.

As the days wore on, Frank spent a lot of time in his room. He thought about telling his grandfather he wanted out of the Pack, but he knew it wouldn't do any good. The Pack wasn't some club you joined or left on a

whim. Besides, he was already a werewolf. He couldn't exactly go crying to his mother and ask her to make it all better.

And as the days turned to weeks he regretted what he'd done less and less. Stempel had always been a jerk. Maybe he'd gotten just what he deserved.

Frank's hunger returned as well. Every night he stared at the moon, and every night he saw that the moon was getting bigger and bigger. Soon it would be completely full. And soon he wouldn't be able to fight the hunger.

The evening of the thirtieth was rainy and unpleasant. Yet somewhere above the mass of dirty black clouds the full moon was shining.

All day long Frank had been in a frenzy. He'd barely been able to keep himself from climbing the walls at school, and as soon as darkness fell, he put his robe on and hurried down to the basement. His mother had already gone to bed. She always went to bed early on nights when the Pack met.

The other members of the Pack began to arrive one by one. They all greeted him warmly and shook his hand. Then they explained some of the finer points of being a werewolf. Frank was told that he'd eventually learn to control his transformations, although he'd never be able to stop himself from turning any later than midnight on the night of a full moon. He was having enough trouble suppressing the change now, and it wasn't but half past eleven.

The men also told Frank that he'd become more powerful as time went by. Someday he might even become a master werewolf like his grandfather, with the ability to talk while transformed.

"Your grandfather is very pleased that you've joined us," said a big-nosed man named Spivy. "It means so much to him after the pain your father caused him."

Frank was confused. "How did my father cause Gramps pain?" he asked.

Gramps walked into the room, and Spivy seemed to shrink.

"I meant to say the pain caused by your father's death . . . at such a young age," he quickly corrected.

Gramps fixed Spivy with a long, hard stare.

"Oh," Frank said, not entirely convinced that the man had merely misspoken.

"Let's get this meeting started," someone shouted.

The beer was flowing in short order, and before long everyone became loud and boisterous. Gramps banged the table with his horn gavel and rose from his chair. "Tonight," he announced, "we must prepare for the 'Feast of the Blood Moon'."

He went on to explain that, because of some unusual astronomical and atmospheric conditions, the moon was going to appear to

turn a dark shade of crimson. Apparently this rare phenomenon had been symbolic to werewolves for centuries.

"We must commemorate the Blood Moon with a sacrifice of the innocent," Gramps proclaimed.

Two large cages hung from the ceiling of the basement. Frank assumed that this was where the innocent sacrifices would be kept until the night of the feast, which would be at the end of the following month.

"Tonight we hunt," Gramps continued. "Tonight we capture the sacrificial lambs. And next month we put them to slaughter."

Frank knew that his grandfather hadn't meant that the Pack was going to go out and capture a flock of wooly lambs. But it didn't matter. The hunger was raging, and the basement soon erupted with howling as the gruesome transformations began.

Like before, Frank didn't remember much after the change. He ran along as the Pack again tramped through the woods and scurried across backyards. They smashed through another door and he saw the terrified faces of a man and a woman surprised in their own bedroom. And there was another sea of red, spilling everywhere and staining everything.

But then there was something more. Something he saw later that morning in disturbing dreams. A couple of the werewolves carried something away from that house. They dragged a boy and a girl right out of their beds, and took them back to the meeting room in the basement.

Frank saw the humans suspended by their pajamas from monstrous teeth, their frail bodies gripped in vicious claws. But he didn't see the victims' faces. Instead he saw only the hideous faces of his comrades, with their normally snarling mouths twisted into demonic smiles. They were in a frenzy of gluttony, their yellow eyes lolling and their bloody red tongues wagging.

When Frank woke up he felt panic-stricken. He was desperate to get to school. He ran the whole way. And, when he got there, he ran up and down the halls, asking people if they'd seen Sally and John.

But the Barrow siblings hadn't shown up for school that morning.

Frank knew the door would be locked, but he had to find some way to get into the basement. Without offering an explanation to anyone he left school and went straight home. He got a crowbar from the shed and pried at the cellar doors with all of his strength. At last there was a splintering of wood and the doors flew open.

He stared into the blackness below and took a deep breath. *What're you afraid of?* he asked himself. *After all, you're the monster here.*

He crawled through the cellar and down into the basement. He rushed into the meeting room and saw that the cages hanging from the ceiling now imprisoned a boy and a girl. His worst fear was realized. The kids in the cages were his two best friends—Sally and John Barrow. They were terrified and sobbing. They looked at him with desperation in their eyes.

Frank started to say something, but Sally shushed him.

"He'll hear you," she whispered. "He's coming back."

Frank heard the loud footsteps of someone coming down the stairwell.

"I'll be back for you," he mouthed to his friends and rushed out of the room.

He darted through the darkness and climbed back up through the cellar, hoping desperately that he wouldn't be seen. Then he disguised the damage he'd done to the cellar doors as best he could and hurried away.

Frank's stomach was twisted in knots. He felt so guilty he couldn't even think straight. No harm would come to his friends until the Feast of the Blood Moon. But the Feast of the Blood Moon would be both the most horrific night and the last night of Sally and John Barrow's lives. Frank had less than a month to find a way to set them free.

The police discovered the badly mauled bodies of Sally and John's parents the following day. Then a frantic search for the children began. But no one would ever think to search the basement of one of the community's most highly respected citizens.

Days and weeks seemed to slip by in a nightmare fog. Frank waited for an opportunity to sneak down to the basement and set his friends free. His grandfather never left the house. And even when the old man was sleeping, Frank couldn't be sure there wasn't some other member of the Pack hiding in the shadows of the basement.

But one day, when Gramps said he was going downtown to conduct some business, Frank decided he simply had to try to release his friends. Time was running desperately short. He fetched the crowbar and crept through the cellar again, making his way down into the meeting room.

Sally jumped up and grabbed the bars of her cage. "Where have you been?" she demanded.

"We thought they'd killed you!" John called from his own cage.

"I came as soon as I could," Frank said. "I'm gonna try'n get you out of here."

He began prying at the bars of Sally's cage, but the bars didn't budge.

"Why don't you just call the police?" Sally asked. "Your grandfather and those other people: they're some kind of monsters!"

"I can't call the police," Frank said. "I just can't. But I'll find some other way. I'll be back soon. I promise."

"Hurry, hurry!" John and Sally pled. They were both becoming hysterical.

When the moon rose that night he saw that it was nearly full. But worse yet was the fact that the normally yellowish surface of the orb now appeared to have turned crimson red. The Feast of the Blood Moon would take place the following night.

The sun rose and slowly began to set, and still Frank hadn't a clue as to what he should do. He became desperate. He could already feel the change taking place inside of him. The hunger was returning.

He had to break Sally and John out of their cages before midnight, or it'd be too late. In a panic he rushed down to the basement and began pulling on the bars with his bare hands.

"That won't work," Sally said.

"Yeah," John cried. "You couldn't even bend them with that crowbar."

Frank ignored them and kept pulling. His heartbeat was racing and he was breathing through his mouth. He knew that darkness was falling. The other members of the Pack would soon arrive.

"What's wrong with your face?" Sally suddenly asked.

"Nothing," Frank replied, his voice little more than a throaty growl.

He glanced down at his hands. His fingernails were growing into sharp claws and little hairs were springing up all along his arms.

Sally screamed.

"You're one of them!" John yelled.

Frank resisted the transformation with all the willpower he possessed. Then he gave the bars another try. This time he was able to bend them quite easily, and within seconds both Sally and John had enough room to squeeze out of their cages. Yet neither of the two siblings moved.

"Come on," Frank growled. "I'm not going to hurt you!"

Sally and John squeezed between the bars, and Frank led them out through the cellar.

"Now get out of here!" he told them. He could feel himself losing control as his body yearned to complete its transformation. "Run!" he snarled at his friends. "Run away from here as fast as you can!"

Sally and John quickly disappeared into the night.

Frank closed the cellar doors and turned around to find all the other members of the Pack surrounding him in a semicircle. They

were dressed in their robes and staring at him with menace in their eyes.

Gramps stepped forward. "Frank," he said. "I'm very disappointed."

"I knew we shouldn't have let him join," said Spivy. "Like father, like son."

"Shut up, Spivy," snapped Gramps.

"What's he talking about?" Frank demanded. "What did my dad do that was so bad?"

"He broke the by-laws of the Pack," said Spivy. "He didn't have the intestinal fortitude to slay humans. He became a no-good cattle mutilator, feeding on the local livestock instead of hunting with his comrades."

Frank was shocked and horrified. It hadn't occurred to him that his father had been a werewolf as well. "You killed him, didn't you? He wasn't evil like the rest of you, so you all murdered him! Just like we murdered Sally and John's parents!"

"No, Frank!" Gramps protested. "That's not true. Your father was shot and killed by a rancher."

"But we should have killed him," said Spivy. "He was a danger to us all. And now his son is the danger!"

Spivy and the rest of the Pack began closing in on Frank.

"No!" Gramps commanded. "Stay back! It doesn't have to come to this."

But there was no stopping Spivy and the others. They began to change more rapidly than Frank had ever seen. Their bodies twisted and contorted, their scraggly hair shooting out like ragweed. Then the razor sharp teeth and claws sprang forth like hundreds of deadly switchblades. They advanced as one snarling body.

"No!" Gramps growled, also morphing into his werewolf state. "I won't let you harm him."

"He's betrayed us," snarled Spivy. "It must be done!" With that, he leapt at Frank.

But Gramps snatched the other werewolf's wiry body in his powerful claws and pulled it out of the air. The rest of the Pack howled in protest, but they couldn't stop Gramps as he flipped Spivy over and tore open the younger monster's bony ribcage. Spivy howled in his death throes as his internal organs spilled out of his body in a gush of blood and guts.

Once they'd recovered from the initial shock the others started to move in on Gramps. Then one of the larger werewolves rushed forward and bit him on the neck. Gramps howled in pain and returned the bite, nearly separating his opponent's head from its hairy shoulders.

Frank could feel his body completing its own transformation. Instinctively, he moved forward to help his grandfather, but Gramps pushed him back.

"No!" he shouted in his raspy voice. "Get out of here! Get out of here and never come back! I can't hold them off much longer."

Just as Gramps finished speaking, another werewolf jumped on his back and started snapping at his face. Gramps hurled the smaller creature across the room, but two others instantly took its place.

Frank's grandfather was struggling for his very life, yet Frank knew he wasn't powerful enough to help him. He was acting almost entirely on instinct, and his every instinct told him to flee.

He scurried up through the cellar and into the night. He ran through the woods, vaulting over the logs and splashing across the streams. His half-animal brain was fevered and unable to focus itself. But Frank still knew he'd always be a creature doomed to the darkness—crawling over fields and pastures, sneaking through backyards and back woods, forever alone . . . and forever cursed.

FOUR

The Unfortunate Invitation

Ryan Carver liked to tease his sister and play a lot of cruel pranks. He threatened to behead her Barbies and swore he'd send her plastic ponies to the glue factory. He even kidnapped her teddy bears and held them all for ransom.

But when he was in a particularly mean mood, he'd make up stories to frighten her. The silliest yarn about a ghost or a bogeyman would send her shivering under her blankets. This made Ryan smile. He considered his sister a pest, and wanted to make her as miserable as possible.

One evening Ryan was reading in his room when his sister knocked on the door.

"What do you want now, Annie?" he asked rudely, not even looking up from his comic book.

"There's a man outside in the woods," she explained, her voice trembling. "I can see him from my bedroom window."

Ryan cast aside his comic book and followed Annie back to her bedroom. *This oughta be good*, he thought. *I've got her so scared, she's imagining things.*

Annie's bedroom was on the second floor and had a big window that opened out on the backyard. The yard sloped steeply away from the house and ended in dark woods.

"There," Annie said, pointing into the thicket of trees. "That's where I saw him."

"Well, there's no one there now," Ryan said.

It was autumn. The wind was rustling in the fallen leaves and sighing through the barren branches. But the woods were completely deserted.

"He was there a minute ago," Annie insisted. "He comes out of the woods every night to stare up at my window. Sometimes he scurries up the trees like a spider, grins at me, and shows me his pointy, white teeth."

Ryan smiled to himself. He was convinced that his sister's imagination was playing tricks on her. And he wasn't about to let such a golden opportunity to have some fun at her expense pass him by.

"So," he said, doing his best to sound concerned. "You say he has pointy teeth. What else does he look like?"

All in one breath, Annie described what she'd supposedly seen. "He's dressed all in black," she began. "And his face is white like a dead person's. His eyes are yellow and diamond shaped. And when he wants to scurry up into the trees, his arms and legs shoot out, with yellow claws on the hands and feet."

"Well, Annie," Ryan said thoughtfully. "It sounds to me like what you've got there is a regular old fiend."

Annie stared up at her brother with wide eyes. He could tell she was very frightened, but as usual this didn't stop him from tormenting her some more.

"Honestly, sis," he told her, "I don't think you have anything to worry about. You see, a fiend can't come inside a house . . . unless, of course, someone who already lives in the house invites him in."

Ryan gave his sister a sinister little smile. She knew what he was about to do too, and tried to block his path to the window. But it was no use. He brushed her aside as easily as he did when she was trying to protect one of her dolls. He unfastened the latch and threw the sash up with a flourish.

"Hey, Mr. Fiend!" he called into the night. "Come on in, you blood-sucking ghoul, you! Annie's waiting for you. She's having a tea party with her bears and dolls tomorrow. You can come if you like."

Instantly, Annie was reduced to tears. "Stop it, Ryan! Stop it!" she pled.

But Ryan felt he was on a roll.

"My name's Ryan Carver, and I live here too. I'm cordially inviting you to come on in and make yourself nice and cozy. You hear that, Mr. Fiend? Our home is your home!"

Annie shrieked and fled the room. At first Ryan was very pleased with himself, but then he became frightened she might summon their mother, so he slinked back to his own bedroom.

"That should teach her a lesson," he muttered to himself, and picked up his comic book again.

For the next several days Annie was uncharacteristically quiet and stayed mostly out of sight. At first Ryan was glad to be rid of her, but he soon became bored. He decided to see what she'd been up to. He went to her bedroom and peered inside, but his sister was nowhere to be seen.

Instead there was a mountainous jumble of dolls and bears heaped upon the bed. This seemed odd, because Annie was particular about keeping her toys in order. The lifeless eyes of the stuffed creatures stared eerily up at Ryan, and he started to feel a little worried.

He stepped over to the bed, bent beneath the canopy, and saw that the pile was rising and falling as though something was breathing underneath. He plucked a few bears from the top of the pile, and uncovered his sister's freckled face. Her eyes were closed. She'd buried herself beneath her fluffy friends.

"What are you doing, weirdo?" Ryan asked.

Annie opened one blue eye, then the other. "I'm hiding," she whispered.

"Why?" Ryan had completely forgotten about his sister's imaginary fiend.

"Because you invited him into the house," Annie said. "Last night he was on the roof trying to find a way in. I heard him scrambling around. Then he climbed down and pressed his white face up against my window."

Ryan laughed. He couldn't believe she was still so frightened over the monster she'd imagined seeing in the woods. *My stories must be giving her nightmares*, he thought.

"It's not funny!" Annie cried. "He looked in my window a long time, just staring and grinning at me."

"Well, maybe I'll leave a window open for him some night," Ryan said. "Then I'll be rid of you for good."

"Don't you dare!" his sister screamed, and buried herself in bears again.

Ryan went back to his own bedroom, played a few video games, and read some more comic books. Then late in the evening, as was often his habit, he fell asleep reading.

When he woke again, deep into the night, his room was pitch dark. This was odd, because he was certain he hadn't turned the light out.

"Light bulb must've burned out," he muttered to himself.

But then he got the distinct impression he wasn't alone. The window was ajar— although he knew he'd shut it earlier—and the curtains were making a whispery sighing sound as they rose and fell from the chilly breeze.

"Who's there?" Ryan called, scanning the darkened room.

There was no answer.

Immediately he began to feel foolish. All of Annie's talk of a fiend in the woods, as well as his own stories, had made him paranoid. He lay back and tried to relax.

He stared up at the ceiling, and suddenly swore he saw it move. Or so it seemed, because something was up there among the shadows—something large, fluttering and scurrying about. Ryan was frozen with fear. And as his eyes slowly adjusted to the darkness he found himself looking up into a cadaverous white face with bright yellow eyes.

The fiend, shrouded in black, smiled down at Ryan, revealing two rows of sharp, jagged teeth. It clung to the ceiling with clawed hands and feet, and Ryan saw that its head was twisted completely backward like that of an owl.

The door creaked open, and Annie appeared silhouetted and framed in the doorframe. Ryan was too scared even to call out to her, although he could tell she was hugging one of her bears.

"You were right, Ryan," she told him. "It turns out I don't have anything to worry about. After all, you're the one who invited him in."

At that she hurried down the hall and back to her own bedroom.

Ryan opened his mouth to call after her, but didn't manage to get the words out. There was another great fluttering and down came the smothering blackness. Ryan's screams were muffled, and the last thing he saw was the horrible white face with its yellow eyes and sharp, smiling teeth.

FIVE

Devil from the Sky

I used to hang out with a bad crowd, and we did a lot of stuff of which I'm not too proud. We picked on smaller kids and pulled all kinds of practical jokes. We put firecrackers in people's mailboxes and left flaming bags of dog doo on their doorsteps. And during Halloween, no jack-o'-lantern was safe from our stomping, smashing sneakers.

There was Jim Penny, Darrel Timlin, Mike Slapper, and me, Charlie Coleman—I still went by Charlie in those days. We were all thirteen or fourteen and pretty mean.

But it was Mike's older brother, Tom Slapper, who was the worst by far. Tom was a few years older than the rest of us, but he sure didn't act like it.

Early one autumn, as the leaves were carpeting the sidewalks in red and gold, Tom

found himself in the worst trouble of his life. The principal was about to kick him out of school. Tom had flushed a cherry bomb down one of the toilets in the boy's bathroom, and the resulting explosion of water flooded half the building. It was an old trick, but I guess the principal had never played it when he was a kid—if he was ever a kid—and he didn't find it very funny.

I was crossing the track field, on my way back from gym, when I saw Tom leaving Principal Doran's office. I caught up with him and asked him what had happened. "I'm suspended," he said. "Just three days, but he really wants to kick me out for good. Expulsion, you know. He says if I slip up just once more . . ."

"Oh, so you got the 'this is your last chance' speech," I said.

Tom flashed his most mischievous smile and his steely blue eyes gleamed. "And that wasn't all," he added. "He laid it on real thick, asking me if I was ever gonna grow out of this sort of stuff."

We walked past the janitor. He gave us the evil eye and slopped his mop down into its bucket.

I couldn't help but think that Doran maybe had a point about Tom. I mean the kid had already been held back two school years, not because he was dumb, but because he was always ditching class and getting in trouble. Did he really think he could keep goofing off and pulling pranks until he was twenty, thirty, or even forty?

Of course I didn't tell Tom what I was thinking. It's a hard thing to tell your friend he's on the wrong path. Even then I guess I wasn't so good at it. And as it turned out, Tom wasn't the only member of our little gang who got in trouble that year. In fact, it wasn't long before we were all in hot water.

Someone with really bad intentions started pulling off all kinds of insane stuff. Naturally the entire town blamed the five of us. At first it all seemed pretty mild—a few garbage cans were turned over, a few fire hydrants were turned on, and Mrs. Millican's poodle was stuck on top of a telephone pole. Well, okay, the poodle on the phone pole was pretty bad. But the fire department got it down quick enough. And the whole experience seemed to cure the little flea bag of its barking addiction. In fact, I think the only noise the dog made the rest of its life was a pathetic whimper.

The pranks were clearly becoming both more vicious and more elaborate. How anyone seriously believed we could be behind it all was beyond me. There were only five of us. It would have taken an entire circus of demented clowns to pull off everything that was going down. Yet people remained convinced we were the culprits. The cops put

Tom on notice, and the neighbors were after our parents to keep better tabs on us.

Then things got really weird. People started complaining about something pounding on the roofs of their cars as they drove down Miller Road just outside of town.

The police accused us of throwing rocks, but they had no proof. Besides, even we knew how dangerous it was to throw rocks at cars.

The cops soon learned that Miller Road was only the beginning. As the weather got colder things just kept getting weirder.

Late one night a man saw something shadowy running along the rooftops and springing from house to house. And there was the guy who got an unpleasant surprise when he went up on his roof to adjust his satellite dish. He came face to face with something he couldn't describe. He tried to describe it on the five o'clock news, but the reporter could only prompt him to choke out the words "It was . . ." Then the poor fellow broke down sobbing. He ended up in the looney bin. But no one really thought he was crazy, because everyone had heard the laughter.

It was horrible and deranged. It seemed to erupt out of the darkened sky over the top of your house, and it sent you cowering under your blankets.

"If this is a hoax," Tom Slapper declared. "It's gotta be the greatest hoax of all time."

Tom had become obsessed with the Harper's Wood Prankster, as they were calling it on the news, and he was determined to catch a glimpse who or whatever was behind it all.

"I heard that crazy laugh last night," Darrel Timlin said.

Darrel was the youngest member of our circle, and he was always striving to prove himself.

"Were you scared, Timlin?" Mike goaded. "Did you call your mommy?"

"No, I wasn't scared," Darrel insisted. "I even wanted to run out and see what it was, only I couldn't find my . . . mittens."

Darrel turned red in the face, as we all laughed at his unintentional admission to wearing mittens at the age of thirteen.

"Well, don't worry," Tom told him. "You'll get your chance to see this thing, whatever it is."

"What do you mean by that?" I asked.

Both Slapper brothers smiled. That was never a good sign.

"Me and Tom have an idea," Mike said.

"What is it?" I asked, my nerves on edge.

"We're gonna stake out the bell tower," Tom explained. "And see this thing up close and personal."

There was no arguing with them. They had already made up their minds. And if any

of us tried to back out we'd be labeled as sissies for the rest of our lives—or at least as long as we lived in Harper's Wood.

So we armed ourselves with an arsenal of BB guns, rocks, and bottle rockets. And when the Saturday evening shadows began to stretch across town we made our way to the old bell tower.

The old bell tower was the tallest building in Harper's Wood. It was considered a historic monument, even though the three bells were cracked and hadn't been tolled in many years.

We crept around back, pried a few boards loose, and jumped in through one of the windows.

"Are you guys sure this is a good idea?" Darrel asked.

The Slappers glanced at one another and smirked. "Why, Timlin?" Mike prodded. "You gonna back out?"

Darrel ignored him and started up the stairs. We all followed, dragging our arsenal behind us in duffel bags. I even had my slingshot and a pocket full of cherry bombs.

The belfry was cold. The floor was littered with loose debris and bird droppings. Ten feet above our heads hung the bells, all corroded and cracked. They were so big, all five of us could have fit easily into the largest. We craned our necks, staring up into them, but couldn't see anything for the shadows. Thick ropes hung from the bells and dangled all the way down through the heart of the tower.

We cleared off a spot on the floor and settled in to wait, feasting on a box of Hostess Zingers.

The view was spectacular. We could see the whole town and the woods that gave Harper's Wood its name. Not to mention the dreaded Miller Road. We saw the lights come on in the houses and kept watch until they went out again. Then there were only the yellow pools of light under the street lamps and the pale glow of the moon.

For a long time nothing happened. We spoke in whispers and finished our Zingers, and still nothing happened. After a while the excitement began to wear off. That's when the Slappers started to get bored. And there was nothing more dangerous than two bored Slapper Brothers.

I saw Tom and Mike eyeballing Darrel and whispering to one another. Darrel was the only one of us who was still afraid. He seemed jumpy—even jumpier than usual—as if he expected the Prankster to spring into the belfry at any moment.

"Hey, Darrel," Tom said. "I dare you to ring the bells."

Darrel was startled. He looked as though a pirate had just ordered him to walk the plank.

"They're not supposed to get rung," I said. "They're too old."

"So what?" Mike groaned. "So what if we even break them? No one ever rings them anyway."

"Come on, let's wake this town up," Tom said. He had that familiar glint in his steel blue eyes. He knew just what buttons to push. "Unless of course you're scared, Timlin. Unless you wanna go home to your mommy and—"

"Okay, fine," Darrel said. "I'll do it." He stood up. He'd taken the bait.

He stepped over to the ropes and paused.

"Go on, man," Mike urged.

Darrel reached up, grabbed one of the thick ropes and gave it a tug. The bell gonged. It was a hollow sound that didn't travel far beyond the belfry.

"Oh, come on," Tom said. "You've gotta put your weight into it."

This time Darrel took a deep breath. Then he gathered all three ropes into his hands and pulled them as hard as his strength would allow. But whether or not the ringing of the bells was very loud I honestly can't say. All I heard—all any of us heard—were Darrel's screams.

Something black and ominous flew out of the largest of the three bells, snatched the unlucky kid up, and shot out of the belfry with superhuman speed.

We didn't see the thing clearly. It was little more than a blur of leathery wings. But it carried Darrel up into the sky until they were silhouetted together against the face of the moon. We could make out Darrel's form. He looked limp and lifeless, like a mouse caught in the talons of a bird of prey. Then there was the thing, with its great black wings and its twisted body.

Panic seized us and we practically fell all over ourselves running down the stairs.

We left most of our weaponry in the tower and ran out into the cold night, searching the sky for any sign of poor Darrel.

But we didn't find him in the sky. We found him in a tree. He was half out of his gourd, but still breathing. Jim Penny and I climbed up and pulled him down.

"What happened?" I asked, when he was able to sit up and clear his head a little.

"It dropped me," he croaked. "It flew me a mile high and back again. Then it laughed right in my face and dropped me in the tree."

"So what was it?" Jim asked. "What was that thing?"

"It was the devil," Darrel told him.

Needless to say we were all pretty freaked out. Darrel was lucky to be alive.

Now I just wanted to go home, lock all the doors and windows, and crawl into bed. And I think I could say the same for the rest of the guys. All of them, that is, except for Tom.

He wouldn't leave Darrel alone. He wanted to know all about the thing. How fast it could

fly. Where it had gone. And most importantly what it had looked like.

Darrel just kept giving the same answer over and over. "It was the devil," he told Tom. "It was the devil." But that wasn't good enough for Tom Slapper.

"We've gotta catch up with this thing," he said, his eyes aglow. "I have to see it for myself."

That's when we heard the laughter off in the distance. It was shrill and awful, but not so far away that Tom didn't want to follow it. And before any of us could tell him he was crazy, he took off running towards the terrifying sound.

"Come on, you guys," Mike said, almost pleading. "We can't let him go by himself."

Darrel was in no condition to go anywhere but home. He said he could make it on his own. The rest of us decided to play follow the leader. I suppose it's difficult to believe, but that was how we felt about Tom. We looked up to him and trusted him. And we figured nothing could harm us as long as we stuck together.

We chased after Tom, running in single file. We chased him and he chased the Prankster. We ran through back yards and jumped fences. We called his name and heard that demented cackle.

Finally we caught up with him at the edge of the woods. He was peering into the dark, trying to see something in the blackness between the trees. He motioned for us to come closer.

"I think I see it," he whispered.

At first I couldn't see anything at all. We stood frozen a long time. Watching.

Then something moved. A shadow. A fluttering of wings. And the laughter erupted from deep in the woods.

Tom took off again, darting in between the trees.

"No, Tom!" Mike yelled. But, as usual, he followed in his brother's footsteps.

I started after him too, but Jim stood rooted in the clearing. I stopped and glanced over my shoulder at him.

"There's no way I'm going in those woods," he said. "And if you go in there after them you must be as crazy as they are."

I did go after them. And from five we were whittled to three. I still had my sling-shot in my hand and a cherry bomb in my jacket pocket. We crunched over the brittle underbrush, our white sneakers streaking through the darkness. Mike kept calling to his brother, who was several yards ahead.

That's when it happened. I knew it was there. I could feel it watching us from high above. Then there was a rustling in the tree-tops and it came swooping down in a shower of wet leaves.

I fell over backward. Mike fell forward and landed face-down. I had the wind knocked out of me and managed to lose my slingshot.

Then I saw the Prankster. I came face to face with the devilish creature, as it hovered above me, its wings a blur of motion, like those of an insect. The thing was horrible to look at, with its bony ribcage and crooked horns. It had a long horse-like face, all veiny and black. The lips were pulled back over the rotting teeth and the nostrils were snorting out putrid smoke.

But the creature's eyes were by far its most disturbing feature. Not because they looked so scary, but because they looked so human. They were bloodshot and seemed to stare straight into your soul. Otherwise they looked just like the eyes of anyone you might meet.

Those eyes locked onto mine and the Prankster laughed that earsplitting laugh.

I had to cover my ears it was so loud. I curled into a ball and rolled over, landing on top of my slingshot. I grabbed the weapon just as the Prankster spread its wings and rose ten, twenty, thirty feet in the air. It was preparing to swoop down on me again, maybe for the kill this time.

The wingspan was incredible—the length of a school bus or more. The thing had the legs of a goat, shaggy and bowed with cloven hooves. And its arms were like long sticks, topped with three sharp claws on either hand. The Prankster began to click those claws and they sounded like rusty iron.

I fumbled in my pocket and dug out the cherry bomb.

The Prankster threw its head back and laughed once more. It would fall on me in seconds.

I fumbled in my pockets again and realized I didn't have any matches. "Mike!" I yelled. "Match! Now!"

The Prankster spun in the air, clicking its claws like mad. Mike scrambled forward, a match cupped in his hand. He touched the small flame to the fuse and the cherry bomb sputtered to life.

The Prankster made its dive, screaming and laughing all the way.

I put the little firework in the slingshot and let it rip. The cherry bomb met the Prankster halfway and exploded in its ugly horse face. There was a familiar flash of pink light and smoke. I think it was the light that did the trick. Those bloodshot eyes, so accustomed to the dark, simply couldn't take it.

The Prankster shot backwards like a cannonball, snapping tree branches in its wake. The demented laughter had turned into a high-pitched scream.

Mike and I looked at one another. We both knew it was time to find his brother and get out of Harper's Woods.

Unfortunately Tom was nowhere to be found. We searched all around, calling and calling for him, but he never answered.

Then we began to notice furtive movements up in the trees. We craned our necks and saw dozens of moving shadows. That's when we realized there wasn't just one devilish prankster in Harper's Woods—there were dozens of them.

They were watching us with those all-too-human eyes. We could make out the sharp angles of their folded wings. They fluttered ever so slightly, ready to unfurl in a split second—a split second that would spell our doom.

I started creeping back toward the clearing.

"Wait," Mike hissed. "We can't leave without Tom."

The Pranksters began to giggle. The giggles grew louder and soon erupted into shrieks and cackles. That was too much for poor Mike. Even the thought of leaving his brother alone in those woods wasn't enough to keep him from hauling you-know-what all the way back to the clearing.

We ran all the way home. We locked the doors and windows. We crawled into our beds and pulled the covers up over our heads.

Early the next morning they sent a search party out to look for Tom. They had sheriff's deputies and dogs. They had volunteers from all over the county. They combed the woods with sticks from dawn until dusk. They flew helicopters over the tops of the trees and called and called.

But they never found Tom Slapper.

Days and weeks passed, and the search was called off. I don't think Mike's parents ever really forgave him for abandoning his brother in those woods. But I can't say for sure, because my family moved across country the following spring.

I didn't think I'd ever see Harper's Wood again. Nor did I want to. I grew up, went to college, and got a job. I even almost forgot all about that autumn and those awful things. I almost forgot about Tom.

Then it all came back to me one night as I was driving through the state on a business trip. I almost swerved off the road when something landed on the roof of the car. Whatever it was, it began pounding and scratching, and all the memories came flooding back. I swerved right and left. I beeped the horn and slammed on the brakes.

Finally the terrible noises ceased.

That's when it occurred to me that I was driving down Miller Road, right outside of Harper's Wood. I didn't want to stop. But I needed gas. I pulled into the station on the outskirts of town. The roof of the car was a mess—all dented and scratched. I filled up as quickly as I could and paid the attendant.

I realized I was being watched.

It sat perched atop a crooked telephone pole, its head cocked. It was studying me.

The wings, the horse face, the goat legs—they were all as I remembered. I wanted to look away. I wanted to get back in my car and drive as far as it would take me. Yet there was something all too familiar about the eyes of the devilish thing. They were steely blue and had a peculiar gleam. It was as if the Prankster knew me. And I knew him.

In the blink of an eye he was airborne. He swooped up over the town, bound for the belfry. He laughed all the way, the shrill sound erupting over the tops of the houses and rattling the windowpanes.

I got back in the car and drove away. I had appointments to keep. Still I couldn't help but wonder what Principal Doran would say. I imagined the poor old fellow waking up with the cold sweats and the shrill laughter ringing in his ears. And just maybe Mr. Doran would be so bold as to venture out into the night, only to come face to face with a creature that had the legs of a goat, the wings of a demon, the face of a horse, and the eyes of Tom Slapper.

SIX

Vengeance and Wrath

Every school has its misfit—a kid who simply doesn't belong. At Mather Middle School, that kid's name was Cyrus Spoon.

Cyrus had a kind of misshapen head, with a prickly crop of rust-colored hair that resembled porcupine quills. His clothes were old and rumpled. His face was flat and broad. And when he opened his mouth to speak, which he seldom did, you could see he was missing several teeth.

The other kids bullied him a lot. They called him Spooky Spoon and laughed at him behind his back and right in his face. And one kid, a horse-faced boy by the name of John Wesley, liked to punch him on the shoulder and push him to the ground.

Cyrus didn't have any brothers or sisters, and his only real friend was his dog, a hound

mix by the name of Harmon. He didn't have a father, and his mother had to work long hours in order to make ends meet.

He slept in a room way up high in a corner of his creaky old house. Harmon slept and snored on a rug at the foot of the bed. Cyrus was only happy when he was dreaming. And he often dreamt about a pair of twins—a boy and a girl—who said they were his friends. They dressed funny, in drab clothing—mostly black. The girl wore a bonnet of all things, and the boy's collar was white and stiff. They reminded Cyrus of pictures of pilgrims he'd seen in history books.

Cyrus played games with them. He talked and laughed with them. He liked hanging out with the twins, as he came to call them, even though he knew they only existed in his dreams.

However, as pleasant as these dreams were, they always took a strange turn before Cyrus woke up. One minute he was walking with the twins in a moonlit forest. The next minute he discovered he was all alone, with the twins calling to him from somewhere far away.

Their voices sounded desperate. "Cyrus, help us! Come set us free!"

"Where are you?" he yelled.

"We're in the basement," the twins called. "Come set us free!"

Cyrus assumed they meant the basement of his own house—that seemingly bottomless place, so dark and cold, where he almost never went.

"What are you doing down there?" he shouted.

"We're sleeping," the twins said. "We've been sleeping so long. Come wake us, Cyrus."

"But where?" Cyrus asked. "Where in the basement are you? I've been down there. I've never seen you."

The answer always came just as the dream ended. "We're buried," the twins told their friend. "We're buried in our coffins six feet under the floor."

Cyrus didn't care to find out if there was any truth to what the twins told him in his dreams. As much as he liked them, he simply couldn't muster the courage to venture down into the basement. It would take a lot more than a few dreams to make him do that.

One day John Wesley and two other boys chased Cyrus up the old bleachers. The bleachers were a wooden monstrosity that rose up the left side of the gym, like a big creaky staircase that led nowhere. Cyrus only made it halfway to the top before John Wesley grabbed him by the collar. "Where do you think you're going?" he asked Cyrus.

Cyrus struggled to free himself, but soon all three of the kids had a hold of him.

"We've got you now, weirdo," one of them said.

For a few seconds the three boys weren't sure what they were going to do with Cyrus, now that they had him. Then all at once they noticed the gap in the bleachers. One of the boards was missing, leaving an opening about the size of a small person. John Wesley's eyes lit up, and Cyrus knew he was in for it.

"Hey," John Wesley said to his friends. "Let's throw him in."

The next thing Cyrus knew, he was lifted up and turned upside down. Then they started stuffing him head first into the dark space where the board was missing.

The entire gymnasium erupted in laughter. All the kids who were jumping rope, or running laps, or just sitting on the parquet and talking, stopped what they were doing to gawk and jeer. "So long, Spooky Spoon," they shouted in chorus.

Where Coach Miller was, the devil only knew.

Cyrus found himself plummeting through a canopy of spider webs, cob webs, and dust. Then he hit the floor with a painful thud. Every bone in his body ached, and he figured it would be a miracle if he hadn't broken anything.

"They're crazy," he said to himself. "I could've broken my neck!"

It was very dark underneath the bleachers, but he knew he was lying in grime and filth. He heard rats chattering in the corners. He stood up and brushed himself off as best he could. The laughter was more distant now. Cyrus bit his lip, determined not to cry.

Then he heard another familiar sound—
that of the bell ringing. It was time to change
classes. The laughter died away, as everyone
filed out of the gym.

By the time Cyrus managed to climb out
from under the bleachers and clean himself
up a bit, he was fifteen minutes late for class.
His teacher gave him detention. But he didn't
even try to defend himself. He knew the
teacher wouldn't listen to him—no one ever
did.

That night Cyrus was home alone again. His
mother was working late, and Harmon was
out sniffing about in the backyard. Cyrus
went up and laid on his bed. He felt so helpless and angry. He wanted to beat up every
kid in his school, especially John Wesley. But
he knew he couldn't. He was just a weak and
ugly kid.

For once he was glad his mother wasn't
home. He didn't want her to ask how his day
went. He never told her about the things that
happened at school. She just wouldn't understand.

"No one understands what it's like," he
muttered as he drifted off to sleep.

"We understand, Cyrus," said two voices, speaking as one. "We know what it's like to be different from all the others."

Cyrus found himself in a moonlit forest, and realized he was dreaming again. But he couldn't see the twins. "Where are you?" he called.

"We're in the basement," the twins cried. "Come set us free. If you set us free, we'll help you get your revenge."

Cyrus followed the voices farther and farther into the woods. It always seemed as though the twins were behind the very next tree. But they never were.

"You won't find us here," the twins called. "You won't see us ever again, unless you come set us free."

As these words were spoken, Cyrus woke up, his pulse racing. He was frantic over the notion of losing the only friends he ever had. And, if there was any truth in his dreams, maybe he would find something in the basement to help him get back at the kids from school. At the very least, it wouldn't hurt to have a look.

He went downstairs and opened the basement door a crack. The darkness was overwhelming. The silence was unbearable. He opened the door wider and made his way down the steps.

He descended slowly, with each warped board creaking underfoot. But when he got to the bottom, and pulled the string that hung from the solitary bulb, he saw absolutely nothing out of the ordinary. It was the same old basement, creepy and cave-like. The same old junk sat piled in the corners, collecting dust. And he certainly didn't hear anyone calling from under the floor.

Suddenly Cyrus felt very foolish. He turned to head back upstairs.

But then something took hold of him and drew him to a particular spot in the floor. He fetched a pickax, held it in his hands, and just stared at that spot. And, although the pickax weighed almost as much as he did, he suddenly hefted it above his head and brought it down with a rush of dank basement air.

Sparks flew as the iron struck the stone floor. Cyrus swung again and again until he'd busted clean through the slab. Next he went and got a shovel and started to dig. He dug feverishly, heaping the dirt up into huge mounds, until his shovel struck something hard.

He knelt down, deep in the pit, and brushed the dirt away with his hands. He uncovered one coffin, then another. They lay side by side, two modest pine boxes, both wrapped in thick chains.

Cyrus took up his shovel and, after several strikes, managed to break the chains from the first coffin. Then he went to work on the second box, bringing the shovel down so hard that he snapped the tool in two on the last

swing. The shovel's head went clanging to the ground and he was left holding the busted handle. It didn't matter, though. The chains were broken.

He opened the first coffin. Inside laid a girl about his own age. She was dressed in a black dress and bonnet, just as he'd seen her in his dreams. Her pale skin glowed in the dim light. She opened her eyes and smiled.

"Hello, Cyrus. I knew you'd set us free."

The other coffin was pushed open from the inside and a boy clambered out. He wore a black suit, with a stiff white collar. Otherwise he looked just like the girl.

Both the twins stood up in their coffins and smiled at Cyrus, their eyes shining like quicksilver. Then, in the blink of an eye, they were standing up on the edge of the pit looking down.

"Who are you?" Cyrus called up to them. "And *what* are you?"

"My name's Wrath," said the boy.

"And I'm Vengeance," said the girl.

"We're your friends," claimed both twins.

The twins helped Cyrus up out of the pit. Their hands were as cold as the dirt he'd just unearthed them from, and they were incredibly strong. They had very white skin and black circles ringed their silvery eyes.

"How'd you get buried down there?" Cyrus asked.

"Our father buried us there," said the boy called Wrath.

"Your father . . . ?"

"Our father was the goodly Reverend Samuel Spense," said the girl named Vengeance.

"Our father *was* goodly," said Wrath.

"Our mother was goodly, too," added Vengeance.

"We weren't so goodly," said both twins.

"We didn't like to stay in our coffins, even though we were supposed to be dead."

"So he chained our coffins up, and built the house on top of us."

Cyrus couldn't believe what he was hearing. "How long have you been down there?" he asked.

"Three hundred years," said Vengeance. "And we're very thirsty."

The twins licked their lips, and Cyrus saw their teeth. Vengeance and Wrath had razor sharp fangs, each pair about two inches long.

"I know what you are," he shouted. "You're vampires, aren't you?"

"We're very thirsty," the twins repeated.

Suddenly there was a distant howling, and Cyrus remembered he'd left Harmon in the backyard.

"Is that a dog?" Wrath asked, licking his lips again.

"Yes, he's *my* dog," said Cyrus.

"We have to go now, Cyrus," said Vengeance. "But we'll be back in the morning. You'll take care of our coffins, won't you?"

"Yeah, sure, I guess." Cyrus looked down at the yawning pine boxes.

When he looked back the twins were gone. He heard the door bang shut. Then there was an awful racket outside. First came a screeching sound, then a flapping and fluttering, and finally a peel of hideous laughter. The noises seemed to rise up above the house and fade into the night sky.

Cyrus ran upstairs and opened the back door. "Har-mon," he called, "Come here, boy! Come here, boy!"

Harmon bolted from the darkness and ran all the way up to the bedroom. Cyrus found him cowering under the bed, his old tail thumping the floorboards.

"I know how you feel, old boy," Cyrus said. "I think we might just be in it up to our necks this time."

Later on Cyrus cleaned the basement up as best he could. He dragged the coffins up out of the pit, pushed them back in a corner, and covered them with an old tarp. Next he filled the gaping hole with the chunks of stone and loose dirt. Then he noticed the shovel—its wooden handle had snapped in two, leaving the broken ends sharp and pointy. He stashed the now useless tool underneath the steps. Finally he went upstairs and crawled into bed.

The next morning he walked the long way to school, feeling as though he needed time to think things over. "They can't be real," he said to himself over and over. And by the time he got to Mather Middle, he'd convinced himself it was all a hallucination.

Then he ran into John Wesley—quite literally. He turned a blind corner and bumped right into the kid he hated most of all. And, despite the fact that he was twice Cyrus' size, John Wesley crumpled into a ball and went crashing to the floor.

Cyrus was stunned and he stood staring down at the helpless bully. John Wesley looked very sickly. His skin was pale and his eyes were all feverish and glazed over. There were strange marks on his neck too. A couple of little holes he quickly covered with his hand. "What are you staring at, Spooky," he demanded. His voice was weak and quivery.

Cyrus couldn't help but smile. "I'm staring at nobody," he said. "Nobody at all."

John Wesley struggled to his feet. "You keep away from me," he warned and hurried down the hall.

Days passed and more and more kids at Mather Middle began to look sickly. Some of them turned up their collars or wore scarves. But Cyrus knew what they were hiding. He smiled to himself, because they all deserved

it. They'd been mean to him for so long, and now they were paying the price.

Cyrus felt powerful. For the first time in his life he wasn't afraid anymore. "It's time for everyone else to be afraid for a change," he said to himself.

Each night Vengeance and Wrath left the basement and disappeared into the gathering gloom. And each morning they returned, their cherubic mouths ringed in red and their bellies swollen from the night's feasting. They'd say hello to Cyrus, and climb into the safety of their coffins.

The twins were the only friends Cyrus would ever have or need. He watched over them, and made sure no one went near the basement. And some nights, when they weren't out hunting, they sat at the foot of his bed and whispered to him.

"Are those kids at school gonna become vampires, too?" he asked one night.

"Not unless we want them to," said Vengeance. Her face was cast in shadows, but Cyrus could see the crimson stains on her blue lips.

"Right now they're just our food," added Wrath.

Cyrus thought for a minute, then asked, "Do you think I could become a vampire?"

The twins looked at one another. "Maybe someday," said Vengeance. "But for now we need you to watch over us in the daylight."

Cyrus nodded his head and went to sleep.

Half the school soon fell prey to the mysterious illness. Yet, when Cyrus thought about it, he realized there were some kids who never really did him any harm. There were even a few teachers who maybe weren't so bad. But Vengeance and Wrath seemed to become less and less selective in choosing their victims. The not-so-bad were suffering right along with the worst of Cyrus's classmates. A lot of kids weren't even showing up for school anymore, because they'd grown so weak.

The twins had done so much for Cyrus, and he simply didn't see how he could say anything to them. Besides, what could he tell them? That they were claiming too many victims? They *were* vampires, after all.

It didn't take long for people to wonder why Cyrus was the only one who wasn't sick. They stared at him in the halls and in class. And although they'd grown to fear him, they still hated him. After a while, Cyrus began to feel as though his life hadn't really changed at all.

He decided that maybe it was time to have a talk with Vengeance and Wrath. He had to make them understand that they needed to use some self-control.

He went down to the basement at dusk. But the twins were already gone—their coffins stood empty. Cyrus shrugged and turned to leave, but then he saw something stirring underneath the stairs. A pair of green eyes peered out at him, studying his every move. The thing began to growl, and Cyrus jumped back.

Then a funny feeling of familiarity came over him. He called out in a shaky voice. "Harmon? Is that you, boy?"

Cyrus's dog slunk into the light. His old head hung low and his floppy ears almost touched the ground.

"What's the matter, Harmon?" Cyrus asked. "Didn't you recognize me?"

Harmon wagged his tail, as his master patted him on the head. That's when Cyrus noticed the dog's teeth, which were two inches longer than normal. They stuck out of his mouth, two great fangs, pointy and razor sharp.

Cyrus gasped in horror. "What in the world have they done to you, boy!"

Harmon was panting like a mad dog. He turned and bounded up the stairs, his tail wagging crazily. Cyrus ran after him. In the kitchen Harmon didn't stop. He busted through the screen door and ran across the backyard.

Cyrus called after him, but it was no use. Harmon had his sights set on the neighbor's cat. He chased the big tom right over the fence and into the woods. Cyrus had never seen him look so ferocious.

He decided he had to find Vengeance and Wrath. He needed to set a few things straight. They didn't want him to join them and become a vampire, yet they'd somehow changed his dog. Enough was enough. You simply didn't mess with someone's dog.

He walked around for an hour, searching darkened alleys and calling the twins out. They never answered him, though, and he saw no sign of them.

Eventually, he passed a convenience store where a bunch of kids from Mather Middle were hanging out. John Wesley was with them. He was leaning up against a lamp post like it was the only thing that could hold him up. One of the kids saw Cyrus, and they all started to point and shout.

Cyrus decided it was best to avoid them, and broke into a run. They started after him, with John Wesley bringing up the rear. They chased him halfway across town.

Cyrus didn't want to lead the little mob to his own house, yet he needed some place he could hide—some place he was familiar with. He cut across a few lawns and headed for school.

He jumped the fence and landed on school grounds, but several kids were right behind him. They caught up with him outside

the gym. A couple of guys grabbed him and pulled him to the ground.

A few minutes later John Wesley came lumbering up. He looked awful, like he was half-dead. His eyes were all blood-shot, his skin as white as the belly of a fish. He covered his neck with his hand and wheezed horribly.

"You don't look so good, John Wesley," Cyrus said.

"Shut up!" John Wesley cried. "I don't know how, but I know you're causing all this, Spooky."

More kids came running up. They glared angrily at Cyrus.

"What should we do with him?" someone asked.

"Take him in the gym," John Wesley said. "We'll throw him under the bleachers again."

They broke into the gym and dragged Cyrus feet first up the bleachers. He banged his head on every board. Then they shoved him into the same gap they'd thrown him through weeks before. He landed on his back, and his lungs seemed to explode on impact. He couldn't breathe. He couldn't move. He just lay there, trying to get his wind back.

At first it was pitch dark, then his eyes began to adjust. Two black shapes, shrouded and pod-like, hung from one of the boards high above him. They reminded him of something, although he couldn't put his finger on what it was. Then one of them moved—fluttered and flurried—and he realized the shapes above him were shaped like sleeping vampire bats. Only they were much too large to be bats.

The black cloaks parted and two white faces were revealed. They appeared almost angelic—Vengeance and Wrath—peering down at him from so high above. They smiled and came oozing down to stand next to him.

"What are you doing here, Cyrus?" Vengeance asked.

"Some guys threw me down here," Cyrus explained.

"That wasn't nice," said Wrath.

"I know," Cyrus said. "But I'd rather not make a big deal of it. What are you guys doing down here?"

"We were just taking a midnight nap," Vengeance said.

The bleachers above them began to creak and rock. The boys were running up and down in a flurry of excitement. Something new was afoot.

The next thing Cyrus knew a long pole was shoved through the gap in the boards. It shot straight down and missed his head by mere inches.

"What's that?" Vengeance asked, eyeing the pole with mild curiosity.

"That's a pole-vaulting pole," said Cyrus. "It looks like those guys are trying to hit me in the face with it."

The vaulting pole was pulled up and rammed down again. It came even closer to hitting Cyrus' head. But this time Wrath grabbed ahold, and when the kids started to pull it back up, he yanked it back down.

A fat kid came smashing, crashing through the gap in the boards. He landed at Vengeance's feet, his eyes wide with shock and disbelief.

"Juicy," said Vengeance.

And out came the fangs. They pounced like spiders, and sank those razor sharp teeth into the kid's pink flesh. Before Cyrus could even say anything they sucked their victim dry. When they were done all that remained was a deflated skin lying over some bones.

Cyrus had seen enough. He jumped up, fought his way through the cobwebs, and ran out the open end of the bleachers. He hurried around to the front, and saw the kids up on top. They still had a hold of the pole-vaulting pole. They rammed it down again and again, desperate to hit something.

But the twins grabbed on and came scurrying up through the boards like a pair of angry insects stirred from their nest. The kids tried to run, but none of them got very far. Vengeance and Wrath were too fast. They leapt and snatched and feasted. They unhinged their jaws and their mouths widened to the size of footballs. And it was a sticky, gory mess they made of Cyrus' classmates.

Cyrus burst through the gym doors and ran all the way home. The only thing he wanted to do was bar his bedroom door and hide under the blankets. He bustled into the house, bolting the door, and glancing over his shoulder as he headed for the stairs. That's when he tripped over his mom's foot.

He looked up to see her sitting on the sofa in the dark. She was wearing her bathrobe and staring off into space. Her hair was all a tangle.

"Mom!" cried Cyrus. "What are you doing home so early? Did you take the night off?"

"I don't feel well," she said. "I'm very tired."

She looked very pale. And Cyrus noticed how the collar of her robe was pulled up over her neck. He didn't want to do it, but he reached up and gently lowered the fuzzy collar. Beneath it, on his mother's thin neck, he saw the tell-tale marks.

Cyrus felt sick inside. He was so ashamed. How could he have allowed this to happen? His own mom had fallen prey to a couple of blood-sucking parasites. And those blood-sucking parasites happened to be his two best friends.

Vengeance and Wrath had to be stopped. He knew there was no other way. For the first time in his life Cyrus Spoon had to do something . . . and do something soon.

Cyrus sat up all night. He listened to the sounds of the house. He heard the window creak as the twins crawled inside and slunk down to their basement lair.

Cyrus didn't move. In fact he barely breathed. He just waited, silent and still. And when the sun rose, streaming daylight into the room, he went downstairs and took a block from the firewood pile.

He'd seen enough horror movies to know how it was done. A stake through the heart always did the trick. Of course the situation Cyrus faced was a little more difficult. He had two vampires to stake. Two vampires so close they seemed to read each other's minds. If he killed one the other was sure to sense something.

He honed the piece of firewood until it ended in a sharp point. Then he opened the basement door, cringing, as it creaked like the mummy's coffin. The walk down into the darkness seemed to take forever. But he finally reached the bottom. He pulled at the string and turned on the meager light.

The coffins sat nestled in the corner. Cyrus moved toward them, his stake at the ready. Something told him he had to deal with Vengeance first. She was the more powerful of the two—the dominant twin. Wrath would likely be lost without her.

Cyrus raised the lid of her coffin and froze, the stake held high above his head. Vengeance looked so peaceful and so innocent—even kind of pretty. But Cyrus remembered the hideous marks on his mother's neck, and how sickly she had looked. He took a deep breath and drove the stake home.

Vengeance became a writhing, twisted mass of limb, fangs, and snaky hair. Her silvery eyes flashed with rage at the sudden betrayal. She hissed and spit and kicked in her death throes. It was terrible. Cyrus could hardly stand to watch.

But he did watch as Vengeance's body crumbled to dust.

Now he turned to the second coffin, the stake still lodged firmly in his grip. And, with a sharp intake of breath, he threw open the lid.

Nothing. No sleeping Wrath. Not even a scrap of black cloth. Just an empty pine box. Cyrus remembered how quick and silent the twins could be. And before he even had a chance to turn around he felt the rush of air at his back.

Wrath descended on him like an owl swooping down on a field mouse. The stake was knocked from his hand. Then the young vampire grabbed him by the face and squeezed. Cyrus thought the icy fingers would crush his cheekbones, as he was lifted off the floor. He kicked his feet and a gurgling sound rose from his throat.

"You killed my sister!" Wrath hissed. His eyes were like liquid steel. He reeled back and flung Cyrus across the room.

Cyrus landed in a heap underneath the stairs. He was sure his leg was broken. And he felt like he was going to pass out from the pain.

The next thing he knew Wrath was climbing the stairs above him. He heard the footfalls thump all the way to the top. But instead of going up into the house, the crazed vampire slipped between the steps and hung upside down some twenty feet above where Cyrus lay. Then he started walking back down on the bottoms of the steps. His upside down face was all pasty and feverish in the dim light. He smiled maniacally at Cyrus and ran his red tongue over his pointy teeth.

Cyrus wedged himself under the stairs. He had no where else to go. Frantically he scoured the floor with his hands, searching for something, anything he might use to defend himself. He was hoping to find a chunk of concrete left over from his little excavation. Instead his fingers fumbled over a piece of wood. It was the broken handle of the shovel he'd used to break the chains from the coffins.

Wrath was almost on him now. He unhinged his jaw and rushed forward. His mouth looked big enough to swallow Cyrus whole.

Cyrus did the only thing he could do. He held the broken handle in front of him as if it were a sword. Wrath fell on the sharp point and screamed. Then he breathed his last foul breath right into Cyrus' face. The makeshift stake had pierced his evil heart.

Cyrus watched in disgust as the creature decomposed at his feet. When it was over, he sat under the stairs for a long time. He couldn't stop shaking. Yet the nightmare had finally ended. Now things could go back to normal. His mother would be safe.

He climbed out from under the stairs and brushed himself off. Everything would be okay now. That's what he told himself. Then he saw something move over in the corner by the coffins. It stared at him with green eyes and growled a familiar growl.

"It's okay, Harmon," Cyrus said, scooping up the stake again. "It's just me, boy." He moved toward his old dog with cautious steps. He held the stake at the ready, and bit his lip so he wouldn't cry.

Days passed and things did get back to normal. The kids who'd been sick slowly recovered. Cyrus's mom got better too.

The gymnasium murders—as they came to be known—remained unsolved. No one really believed that Cyrus could have done it. After all, he was just a weak and ugly kid.

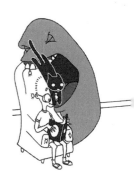

However, people did tend to be a little nicer to Cyrus when it was all said and done. They didn't push him around so much. They didn't make fun of him in front of his face, or even behind his back. After all, there was something strange about that dog of his. Something that made people a little more than uneasy.

That morning in the basement Cyrus killed two of his friends, but found he couldn't harm a third. Just as he was about to bring the stake down, he tossed it aside and patted the old dog on the head.

"It's okay, boy," he told Harmon. "I don't care what they've done to you. You're still the best friend I've ever had."

Harmon wagged his tail and panted. And his three-inch fangs gleamed bright in the pale basement light.

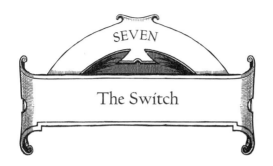

SEVEN

The Switch

When Estelle Parsons was four, she stood in her pajamas and watched her parents lay her baby brother in the crib. Estelle wasn't much impressed with the baby—it only cried and soiled itself and made everyone fuss over it the way the way they used to fuss over her. And though she knew it was wrong, she couldn't help but wish her parents had never brought her brother home from the hospital.

Later on she thought maybe she'd wished too hard. Because when Estelle Parsons was five she stood in her pajamas and watched a shriveled hag snatch her brother from the crib and replace the baby with an exact duplicate. Estelle had no idea who this woman was, yet the hag was standing in the nursery at midnight, wrapping the baby in the folds of her dirty cloak. She had a great hunched

back and a face that resembled that of a jackal. "Now make some mischief in the world," she whispered to the impostor baby.

Estelle gasped in horror, and the stranger turned and fixed her with a stare. Then the old hag raised a warty finger and hissed out the most vicious shush that ever silenced Estelle Parsons.

Only Estelle wasn't silent for long. She yelled for her mother and father as loud as her five-year-old lungs would allow. But by the time her parents came to see what was the matter, the old hag had stepped into the closet and disappeared among the shadows and spider webs.

Estelle's mother gathered the thing—the thing she thought was her baby boy—up into her arms. "Hush, Stella, you'll make the baby cry."

But the baby wasn't crying. In fact, the creature that passed from that day forward as Estelle's little brother didn't do a lot of crying or cooing or any of the things ordinary babies are known to do.

And as the years went by the baby grew into a very unordinary boy.

His name was Eugene, or so everyone believed. He was a stocky boy, with sandy, close-cropped hair. He had a wicked smile and a cruel laugh. He'd flash the smile whenever he gave Estelle a kick under the table where their parents couldn't see. Later on, he'd laugh that laugh, digging little rabbit punches to her kidneys when no one else was around.

Estelle didn't mind the smile or the laugh or even the bullying, so much as she did the one thing her so-called-brother always knew he could do to unnerve her. Eugene's eyes were like little pools of oil, and he could stare at her for hours at a stretch. Nothing Estelle did, no matter how desperate, ever broke his concentration.

One particular afternoon, when Eugene was being especially cruel, she simply couldn't stand it anymore. "Stop staring at me!" she yelled. "I'll tell Mom and Dad if you don't leave me alone."

"Go ahead and tell them," Eugene said in his singsong voice. "They won't believe you. They don't believe anything you say."

Estelle knew he was right. Her parents did often doubt the things she told them. After all, when she was small she'd repeatedly insisted her baby brother had been stolen by an old woman and replaced with an identical who-knew-what. Of course, everyone insisted that had been nothing more than a bad dream.

"It *was* just a nightmare," Estelle told herself time and again. "It's not like Eugene's a monster. He's just mean."

But as Eugene grew bigger and stronger his cruelty seemed to have no boundaries. He

hung out with a nasty bunch of kids—bullies, thugs, and the like. And he was forever whispering in someone's ear, planting the seeds of a fight or plotting some vicious prank. He goaded other kids to lie, cheat, and steal. But whenever anyone got caught he managed to be far from the center of attention.

Late one evening Estelle became all the more convinced that her brother really was a monster. This was the evening on which her friend Ruth Lester ended up with a broken arm.

Ruth was a shy and reserved girl, who took band practice with Estelle. It was on the way home from band practice that the incident occurred. Several boys—friends of Eugene's—began to chase the girls and finally cornered them in front of the cemetery. Then the bullies formed themselves into a semicircle and marched forward, driving the girls into the old boneyard.

Matters were made worse when one boy—a pig-faced little monster—grabbed Ruth's clarinet case from her arms and went darting between the headstones. And, although Estelle tried to stop her friend from doing so, Ruth took off after the thief.

It was growing quite dark inside the cemetery. The trees were great twisted things and the homes of a million shadows. The headstones were little more than chunks of marble and granite, all cracked and scarred. They stuck up out of the ground like the teeth of some giant monster that was trying to eat its way up from the bowels of the earth.

"Ruth!" Estelle cried. "Wait up!"

She finally caught up with her friend deep inside the cemetery. Ruth, who suffered from asthma attacks, was now panting for breath, and there was no sign of the boy who had taken her clarinet. "My parents paid a fortune for that thing," Ruth wheezed.

Then Estelle spotted her brother—her so-called-brother—standing atop someone's crypt, and watching them with his black and expressionless eyes. He put his dirty fingers in his mouth and whistled, and suddenly Estelle and her friend found themselves barraged with a storm of rotten eggs. One struck Ruth right smack in the eye and the stinky yolk oozed down her face.

Eugene's friends had taken positions behind the gravestones and in the shrubs, and were hurling the eggs down on the girls.

"Stop it! Stop it!" Estelle cried.

The boys eventually stopped throwing, but only because they ran out of eggs.

"You make them give it back, Eugene," Estelle shouted to her brother.

"Give what back?" Eugene asked innocently, springing down from the crypt.

"You know what."

Eugene looked thoughtful. "Oh, you mean that girl's clarinet," he said. "Okay, sis. I'll get it back for her." He stuck his fingers in his mouth and whistled again.

The pig-faced boy appeared from behind a large headstone.

"You heard my sister," Eugene said to him. "Give that girl her clarinet back."

The boy strutted toward Ruth, ceremoniously holding the clarinet case in front of him. He offered it to Ruth, but she sensed a trick and was reluctant to take it.

"Go ahead," Eugene urged. "It's what you want, isn't it?"

The other boys could hardly restrain their glee.

"It had better be in there," Estelle said.

"Take a look."

All at once Ruth grabbed the clarinet case and threw it open. She took one glance at what was inside and all the color washed out of her face. Then she dropped the case on the ground and ran screaming into the darkness.

Eugene and his friends erupted in uproarious laughter.

Estelle could see the thing in the clarinet case now. It was pressed in the plush red lining where the instrument was supposed to go. A swarming multitude of ants and maggots were devouring the bits of flesh still clinging to it. It was a human forearm bone.

"You sickos!" Estelle yelled.

She started after her friend, but it was too late. Ruth was so freaked out she didn't look where she was going. Eugene and his friends had robbed a grave in order to get the forearm bone. And they'd left the plot all dug up. Ruth fell right in, breaking her arm on the side of the coffin.

Estelle ran to get help. She had to get her parents. But instead she ran straight into Eugene. "You won't get away with this!" she told him. "I'm telling Mom and Dad."

"Go ahead and tell them," Eugene said. "You know they won't believe you."

Estelle was furious. "I know what you are!" she hissed. It was something she'd never been bold enough to say to his face. "You're not my brother. You're some kind of monster. And I don't know how, but somehow I'm going to prove it."

Eugene smiled at this, as Estelle knew he would. Yet just before she sprinted off to find help for Ruth, she glimpsed something new swimming in the black pools of his eyes. Something that looked very much like fear.

"Maybe I'm not your brother," he called. "And maybe you're not my sister. And just maybe *you're* the one who's the monster."

Estelle ignored him and ran all the way home.

Eugene did get punished, along with a few of his cronies, but the boys weren't the only

ones in trouble. Estelle, and even Ruth herself, were punished right along with the bullies who'd tormented them. As unfair as this treatment may have seemed, however, it wasn't what really upset Estelle. She knew how easily Eugene could twist the facts with his lies.

The thing that really got Estelle, and made her furious, was the mild nature of Eugene's punishment. Ruth's arm got broken because of one of his stupid pranks. And all her parents did about it was ground him for a measly two weeks.

Estelle was grounded too, which meant she had to spend hours upon hours trapped in the house with Eugene. This situation would have been bad enough under normal circumstances. And things were far from normal.

Eugene knew that she knew he wasn't what he appeared. So he didn't bother to pretend anymore. He watched her constantly, as if waiting for the right moment to strike. He hardly ever spoke, but she could tell he was plotting something wicked.

Once she swore she saw golf-ball sized lumps form under his skin. Then his flesh turned purple and veiny, and the lumps moved up and down his arms, neck, and face. It was as though his true shape was bubbling up and about to come bursting through his fake skin.

Estelle didn't get much sleep. Most nights she lay awake in her bed and watched the door, terrified he'd sneak in. When she did finally fall asleep, she had horrible dreams. Eugene would climb through her window, with his face all contorted and twisted, like in a funhouse mirror. Then he'd reach out for her, his hands scaly and black.

Sometimes she didn't know where her dreams ended and reality began. One night she thought she was dreaming, although she could never be sure. Eugene slipped in through the door, and shed his skin like a squirming snake. He took on a hundred different shapes in her nightmares, each more monstrous than the last. This time his body, except for the round white face, was covered in coarse brown hair.

He stretched himself out until he was as tall as the ceiling, with his arms and legs becoming twisted and knotted like the branches of a tree. Then he bent down over her bed and began to smother her with her pillow.

Estelle kicked and struggled, her heart and lungs ready to explode. How could she have been so stupid as to tell him she knew he was a monster? Now he had no choice but to do away with her.

She pounded the wall with her fist, and hoped her parents would hear. This must have scared him, because the smothering ended. Estelle cast the pillow across the room, and sat bolt upright.

There was no one there. Had she been dreaming? She didn't think so. Her door was flung open, and creaking back and forth on its hinges, as though someone had just rushed out.

Estelle knew she had to prove to her parents that Eugene wasn't really their son. She planned to sit them down the next morning. Somehow she would convince them of the truth.

In the meantime, she needed to stay awake and on her guard—all night long if that was what it took. She clutched her blankets up under her chin and waited for the first light of morning. But the night seemed to stretch on and on, and her eyelids began to grow heavy.

She shook herself awake and jumped out of bed. She paced the floor, wishing it were morning, but she knew it wouldn't come for several hours.

After a while she felt thirsty and wanted a drink of water. The kitchen seemed far away, however, and she'd have to walk past Eugene's bedroom to get there.

Of course, she knew she could run to her parents if Eugene tried to get her. That was the one thing that kept her safe. Eugene didn't want to do anything to make Mr. and Mrs. Parsons suspect he wasn't what he appeared. And Mr. and Mrs. Parsons were right down the hall.

Estelle crept down to the kitchen and got her drink of water. Then she hurried back upstairs, scampering past Eugene's bedroom and back into her own.

She shut the door with a big sigh of relief. There was no sign of Eugene.

She felt she could let her guard down. Maybe even rest awhile. Lazily, she turned toward her bed. And that's when she saw it, lying there, stirring beneath the blankets. She froze in place.

Someone else, or something else, was in her bed. It looked to be a girl about her own age, although the room was too dark for Estelle to be sure.

Her first instinct was to run screaming into her mother and father's room. But she didn't do that. Something inside her, something she didn't quiet understand, made her want to confront the person on her own.

She reached for the lamp, turned the switch, and saw that the person lying in the bed was her double, identical to her in nearly every way. The intruder, now bathed in the dull yellow light, sat bolt upright and stared at Estelle with a pair of black and empty eyes. She was even wearing the same pajamas as Estelle.

The real Estelle took a step backwards, horrified and aghast at the creature that had invaded her bedroom. The imposter hissed like a snake. Estelle had seen enough and was

desperate to flee. She turned to run, but found her escape blocked.

She saw movement in the corner by the door. Someone was crouching there, watching her and breathing heavily. Then the thing rose up, snapping and snarling, and Estelle could see it was the old hag who, some twelve years before, had taken her brother and replaced him with Eugene. Her eyes were full of menace and her jackal face was twisted in fury. She leapt at Estelle, her filthy cloak fluttering behind her like the wings of a great black bird.

The lamp flew from the table and the room seemed to tumble. Estelle was knocked to the floor, and the old hag grabbed her by the ankles. Estelle fought like mad, but the hag was too strong. She dragged the girl along the floor toward the closet.

"This is a dream," Estelle told herself. "It's all just a dream!"

The hag opened up her mouth and cackled. Her teeth were all jagged and black. Her breath was like something dead.

The closet door hung open. Estelle was dragged ever closer, the rug burning her back. The hag was tugging so hard, Estelle thought her legs might be pulled apart at the knees. She grabbed for the closet door. She clawed at the wall. She was desperate not to be pulled inside. She knew that if she went behind the coats and dresses, back among the shadows and spider webs and whatever lay behind these, she'd never again see the light of day.

She kicked and punched and bit. She chewed and clawed and spit. She flew into a frenzy, twisting every which way. And at long last the hag's terrible grip was broken.

Estelle leapt to her feet and went hurtling for the door. The hag reached for her. The imposter reached for her. But Estelle lowered her shoulder like a linebacker and knocked them both aside.

Now Estelle was out in the hall, screaming and sprinting toward her mother and father's room. The hallway seemed impossibly long, with the walls and ceiling growing higher, and her parents' bedroom door ever more distant. Yet if she could only make it to the other side of that door the nightmare would end.

Eugene sprang out of his bedroom like a jack-in-the-box with its face all cracked and peeling. The fake skin was falling away, and something monstrous was coming to the surface. He cackled like a wild thing, and tried to grab Estelle.

Estelle screamed with all the power in her lungs, and pummeled his face with both fists. She could feel the fake flesh sticking to her hands, but she didn't want to see what lay beneath it. She'd seen hundreds of Eugene's

horrible faces in her nightmares. Now she didn't care which was the true face. She only wanted to get to the safety of her parents' room.

She kept running.

At long last she reached the door and flung it open. Then she jumped right up on the big bed just as she'd done when she was a little girl.

Her parents began to stir in the darkness. "What's wrong, dear?" her mother asked quite calmly.

"Didn't you hear me screaming?" Estelle said, her heart pounding. "They're after me! Eugene and the old woman and . . ."

Estelle was at a loss to explain how she'd come back to her room to find her double lying in the bed. "I know you won't believe me," she sputtered at last. "But you have to. I wasn't dreaming when I was little. I did see an old woman steal the baby and replace it with Eugene. Now the old woman's come back. She's a witch or something. And this time she's trying to replace me!"

There was a long pause, as Estelle huddled between her mother and father and hoped they wouldn't send her back to her room.

"Mom, Dad?" she pled, her voice quaking. "Please say you believe me. You just have to believe me."

"Of course we believe you, Stella," her father said.

Estelle's heart leapt. She felt overjoyed at the notion that her parents were finally listening to her. And for the first time in a long time she began to feel safe.

"So they tried to get you?" her mother asked. "Eugene, the old woman, and this other you?"

"That's right," Estelle said, wondering how her mother could be so calm when those things were loose in the house.

"Did they try to pull you into the closet?" her father asked.

"That's right," Estelle answered. "But I got away." She tried to make out her parents' faces in the dark. But the adults were just two black shapes sitting on either side of her.

"It's a pity," her mother said.

"Quite a shame," her father added.

Estelle was very confused. Did her parents doubt her again, as they'd done so many times before? Did they think she'd gone crazy and needed to be humored? Or was it something else?

"Mom, Dad," she said. "I'm really scared. Please turn the light on."

"Are you sure you want the light on?" her parents asked. "It's very late."

"Yes," Estelle said. "Please just turn it on!"

Her father reached for the lamp and turned the switch. Orange light spilled out across the bed in a broken circle. Now Estelle

could see her parents' faces and, although she knew there was no one to help her, she began to scream.

They stared down at her with eyes as empty and black as Eugene's. Their faces were veiny and purple, and golf-ball-sized lumps were bubbling up beneath their skin.

"You should have let them take you, dear," the thing in the shape of her mother said. "It would have been much easier."

"After all," her father's replacement added. "Your *real* parents didn't put up much of a fight."

They grabbed her arms, but she didn't struggle. She had no place left to run. And now the others were shuffling down the darkened hallway, making their way toward the light.

"Come in, children," called the creatures posing as Estelle's parents. "We're going to be a family again."

Estelle closed her eyes as the hideous siblings scurried into the room and hopped up on the bed. She could feel them surrounding her, their awful eyes boring in. Then she heard them peeling, ripping, and shedding their fake skins.

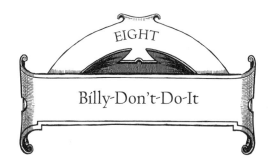

EIGHT

Billy-Don't-Do-It

None of the kids in my hometown were little angels. We got in as much trouble as kids in any town in any corner of the world. But whatever the rest of us did to earn all the punishments our parents and teachers ever doled out never even came close to matching the crimes of Billy Gordon Grubbs.

We called him Billy-Don't-Do-It, because that's what everyone was always yelling at him.

"Billy-Don't-Do-It!" the Wren sisters screamed when he menaced them with a slithering black snake. "Billy-Don't-Do-It!" little Sam Simon hollered, just before Billy got him in a headlock and dug a bony knuckle into his scalp. "Billy-Don't-Do-It!" I shouted, as he toppled the canoe and sent Abigail Stetson, our

picnic lunch, and myself all sinking to the bottom of Sawyer's Pond.

Abigail and I swam to the surface and we were both okay. But a lot of the things that crossed Billy's path weren't nearly so lucky. He seemed to have a personal score to settle with all of nature. He stomped every flower he saw and uprooted entire gardens. He obliterated ant piles and burned rabbits out of their dens. He kicked every dog in town and tried to pick the birds off the telephone wire with his BB gun.

But whatever it was that made him decide to chop down the weeping willow tree nobody knew. Although demonic inspiration was as good a guess as any.

The weeping willow stood in the middle of a clearing in the heart of the forest. The soft branches cascaded endlessly from the trunk, creating layer upon layer of leafy green curtains. Everyone said it looked like a frozen fountain, until the breeze rustled the branches and the leaves began to whisper. The tree had been a popular gathering place for generations. Hundreds of sweethearts had met behind the cascading curtain. Hundreds of flailing forms had danced among the leafy branches.

That is, until Billy-Don't-Do-It took his dad's ax and put a stop to all the frolicking and fun.

The Wren sisters were sitting under the leaves, braiding each other's hair. They watched him slip between the branches. His big face, with its sloping forehead, beady black eyes and drooping jaw, looked like a steam shovel. His tangled brown hair was standing straight in the air, as he swung the ax like an executioner who loves his work. He took ten whacks and the trunk creaked and cracked and finally splintered. Then the venerable tree tottered and fell, the long branches thrashing and crashing to the ground.

None of us had been far from the clearing, and when we heard the chopping of the ax, we all came running. The Wren sisters were crying. We looked at the fallen tree. The leaves had grown still and were already starting to whither. Billy-Don't-Do-It stood in triumph on the stump, holding his ax above his head and pumping his fist at the sky.

No one bothered to ask why he'd done it. He just liked to destroy things. And if someone had tried to tell me that any of those helpless or inanimate things that Billy had hurt would ever get their revenge . . . Well, let's just say I would've had my doubts.

It was fall—a few nights after Halloween— and many decorations were still hanging. Witches, skeletons, and scarecrows gave silent greeting from the front porch of nearly every house. Leftover candy was picked over, thrown out, or finally eaten. Costumes lay crumpled in corners like the shed skins of creatures strange and small. It was a time

when fantasy met reality and the twilight seemed to go on forever.

Billy was laid up with a fever and hadn't managed to make it to school in several days, let alone perform his usual Halloween pranks. So I suppose he didn't put up much of a struggle when they crept in and carried him off into the night. But then I didn't put up much of a fight when they came and got me.

The little noises woke me sometime after midnight. I sat up and swore I saw something move—something in the corner by the door. *There can't be anything there*, I told myself. *I'm acting like a scared little kid. It's just my imagination*. I lay back down and turned toward the wall, determined to go to sleep.

But then the room grew so quiet and still I could hardly stand it. I knew it was silly, yet I couldn't help but feel like something was watching me. *I'll just take a quick peek*, I thought. *Just to prove to myself there's nothing there. Then I'll go right to sleep*.

Very slowly, I rolled over and saw that I had been wrong about some*thing* watching me. There were actually dozens of them. Dozens of eyes—maybe a hundred pairs—staring at me from every corner of the room. They were yellow with red, diamond-shaped pupils. They surrounded me like a galaxy of stars. They gazed down from the ceiling and up from the floor and from all the spaces in between.

I managed to utter a little cry, but then they were upon me. Clawed hands seized my ankles and wrists and covered my mouth. Terrible faces with jagged, beak-like mouths pressed in on me. Their bodies were hairy in some places and leathery in others. "Thomas Grey. Thomas Grey," they whispered. "You're coming with us!"

The next thing I knew, I was lifted on arms as skinny as sticks and carried through the window, my blankets trailing behind. Then dozens of wings—maybe a hundred pairs— unfolded from dozens of hunched backs and we shot into the purple sky. Two of them had me by my feet, and I hung upside down, twisting in the wind. I thought I would pass out as I watched the roof of my house grow smaller and smaller. But I stayed awake long enough to see the chimneys and the church steeple pass below like the masts of Spanish galleons sunken under a sea of night.

Then we were flying over the forest, the treetops a blur of dark color. Suddenly a black circle opened below and, as we descended, I realized it was the clearing where the weeping willow used to stand. The winged things dropped me several feet from the ground and I landed in a pile of leaves, sticks, and stones. Then they took up positions all around the clearing, their wings fluttering and their cruel eyes aglow.

My head was spinning. I looked around and saw that I wasn't alone. Sam Simon was there, sitting in his doctor denims, hugging his knees and shivering. Next to him the Wren sisters still lay in their four-poster, with their nails dug deep into the mattress. (The winged things must have been unable to pry them out of bed, so they'd taken them, bed and all.) Abigail Stetson was there too. Dressed in her pajamas, she sat at the foot of the Wren sisters' bed. She saw Sam and me and motioned for us to come sit next to her.

So there we all were in a big white bed in the middle of a ring of darkened trees and wet leaves, with those awful things staring down on us. "What are they?" I whispered to Sam.

"I'm not s-s-sure," he said. "But I t-t-think they're harpies. In mythology they're blamed for stealing everything that was ever lost and never found."

"S-s-so what do they w-w-want with us?" asked Abigail.

Sam shrugged and that was just as well, because I don't think we really wanted to know why a bunch of supposedly mythological monsters had carried us deep into the woods in the dead of night.

I glanced over at Abigail. She was shivering pretty badly and I was tempted to put my arm around her. But she'd given me the cold shoulder ever since our mishap in the canoe and I thought better of it.

That's when the horn blew and we all just about jumped out of our PJs. It was a horrible noise, as jarring as a foghorn and as sad as the death cry of some wounded beast. As the sound waves reverberated through the trees the forest began to crawl.

Hideous and terrible creatures slithered into the clearing, their scales shining in the scant moonlight. Trolls burst from the ground, clawing forth with their gangly arms and shaking the loam from their humped backs. Little devils with pointy tails and pointy faces appeared from thin air and pointed at us, whispering incantations under their breath. Gnomes and pixies, smaller still, zigzagged from tree trunk to tree trunk. Werewolves trotted from the shadows. Specters floated down from the sky.

The wind blew bitter cold, the leaves crashing like waves on a rocky shore. Mayhem was in the air—and maybe murder.

The clearing was alive with a thousand growls, howls, grunts, and groans. Animal musk filled our nostrils and ectoplasm swirled all around us. Then a very singular creature stepped from the darkness. He was less scary than the others, yet somehow more frightening.

He was old and bent, his legs wooly and haunched, like those of an animal. His cloven hooves clomped the hard ground as he stepped into the center of the clearing. He had the stomach, chest and arms of an ordi-

nary man, but his face was a mix of beast and man, with a short snout and two curved horns that grew right out of his temples. He surveyed the scene with a pair of cobalt blue eyes. Sam didn't have to tell me what he was. I knew he was a satyr.

He climbed up on the stump that was all that remained of the weeping willow tree and raised his hands. "SILENCE!" he bellowed.

The word echoed through the night. All the creepy crawlers froze. Even the crickets went quiet. Then a squat troll blew the horn we'd heard a moment before and all the wild creatures formed a circle within the trees. Two other trolls rolled a boulder up behind the stump, and the satyr perched atop it. Then he spoke again, more quietly this time, but his words were still resonant. "Bring forth the accused."

The troll blew his horn, not so loud this time, but he held the note for several moments. Then there was a commotion in the sky, and four more harpies came flapping down. They carried a bundle of something that was sobbing and kicking weakly. They dropped the load in front of the weeping willow stump and out poured Billy Gordon Grubbs. His sudden appearance elicited a chorus of hissing and low growls from the strange assemblage.

Billy blinked dumbly and looked around. He looked at the satyr and all the other creatures of the night. We could see he didn't want to believe. But then none of us wanted to believe this night was anything but a bad dream.

The satyr raised his hand for silence. He stared down at Billy. "Speak, boy. Tell us your name."

Billy was trembling something fierce, but somehow he managed to utter the words. "B-B-Billy Gordon Grubbs."

The growling and hissing rose up again, and this time the satyr let the wild things have their say. Then he leaned forward until his wrinkly face was less than an inch from Billy's own pale face. He shook his massive head and said, "I asked you to tell us your name, boy!"

Billy looked as though he might cry or even faint. "I already t-t-told you," he insisted. "B-B-B-B-Billy G-G-Gordon G-Grubs."

"No!" roared the satyr. "Tell us your real name. Your true name."

Billy's mouth gaped in his terror and confusion. But every other creature in the clearing knew exactly what the satyr meant. The army of devils, pixies, and gnomes began to whisper. The trolls grunted from deep within their fat bellies. The werewolves snarled and the specters moaned from the treetops. A chorus rose up repeating the same refrain over and over. Even the harpies screeched it from their beaks.

"Billy-Don't-Do-It. Billy-Don't-Do-It! BILLY-DON'T-DO-IT!"

At last they were silent. A freezing drizzle began to fall. All eyes were on the satyr. He spoke slowly and deliberately. "We, the guardians of the forest. We, the keepers of the night. We who protect all that crawls through green grass, scurries on four legs, or grows forth from shoots in the soil hereby call to order the trial of the human boy know forevermore as Billy-Don't-Do-It!"

The horn blew. The crowd roared. And Billy-Don't-Do-It looked over at the five of us, his fellow humans, with desperation in his eyes.

"What do you think it's all about?" I whispered.

"Who knows," Sam Simon said.

Now, I'd known Billy longer than anyone. I think he may have even considered me a friend in his own twisted way. And I can't say I was surprised to see him put on trial. I had always assumed he would end up in front of a judge. Just not a judge with three-inch horns and cloven hooves.

But one question remained if it wasn't a dream. If these fantastic and frightening things really were the guardians of the forest—and I must say I tend to believe the werewolves were simply there for the show—just which one of Billy's many crimes were they actually going to charge him with?

A few seconds later I had my answer.

"Bring forth the victim," commanded the satyr.

Two trolls began to burrow in the dirt around the weeping willow stump. They dug down deep and pulled something to the surface.

Abigail gasped and shielded her eyes. Sam shook his head in disbelief. The Wren sisters burst into tears. It was a heartrending sight. For the trolls had dragged forth the most pitiful and ghastly creature any of us ever laid eyes on. The body looked like a rotten bundle of sticks, although it had skinny arms and legs, each about eight feet in length. But these limbs were all twisted and as brittle as twigs. The poor thing writhed, twisting its small head this way and that. Its eyes were little more than empty knotholes, with a bigger knothole for a mouth that gapped jagged and black. This unfortunate being was something known as a dryad, or tree spirit, and it was slowly dying.

Even the satyr seemed affected by the dryad's suffering. He looked away from the broken stick figure, and his eyes bored once more into the accused. "Billy-Don't-Do-It. You are hereby charged with crimes against beast and fowl, crimes against flora and foliage, crimes against your own species and every species you've ever known. But above

all, you stand accused of murder most base! Murder for murder's sake!"

The chorus rose. "Murder. Murder! MURDER!"

Billy squirmed under the satyr's gaze. But the satyr's gaze remained unbroken. "What say you to these charges? How do you plead?"

"I-I-I . . . " Billy yipped like a kicked dog. "I . . . I didn't . . . I never . . . I mean . . . I . . . Don't I get a lawyer?"

He'd seen enough television shows. I have to hand him that.

The satyr almost smiled—almost. Then he scanned the motley crowd and asked, "Who will argue in defense of this . . . pathetic human?"

A man stepped forward. He wore shining robes and his features were quite handsome, even angelic. "I will argue for the defense," he said in a soothing voice.

"Where'd he come from?" I asked.

But no one answered me, because a second figure had stepped into the middle of the clearing. This time it was a beautiful woman. In fact, she was radiant, and she wore robes of the same material. "And I will argue for the prosecution," she trilled.

The horn blew, and the counsels took their places. The man stood with Billy, while the woman stood next to the dying dryad.

"Now," the satyr began. "How does the accused plead?"

"I'm innocent!" Billy squealed. "Er, not guilty, that is! Innocent! Not guilty!"

Billy's lawyer bent down and whispered something in his ear.

Billy started. "What? Yes! Yes, of course I'm sure!"

The handsome man turned back to the judge and bowed. "My client wishes to plead 'not guilty,' your honor."

A great uproar arose from every throat, fangs were barred, and angry eyes flashed with a hundred shades of red, yellow, and green.

"Very well," the satyr said. "The prosecution may now call its first witness."

The radiant woman approached the stump. "I call forth the human boy known as Billy-Don't-Do-It."

"If *she's* not human," I wondered aloud, "then what is she?"

No one seemed to hear, however, and we all watched in horror and fascination as a pair of trolls dragged Billy forward and deposited him in a circle of stones next to the stump. The woman stood above him and ran her fingers through his choppy hair. "Now tell us, dear boy," she began. "Where were you on the afternoon of October the thirtieth?"

Billy got a dreamy look in his eye and he sounded like someone talking in his sleep. "I was here in the forest," he confessed.

"And did you enter this clearing?" the woman asked, her fingers playing chopsticks on his scalp.

"Why, yes," Billy admitted. "Yes, I did."

"And were you carrying something? A weapon, perhaps?"

Billy closed his eyes, completely spellbound. "Oh yeah, sure," he agreed. "I had my dad's ax."

Everyone and everything in the clearing, with the obvious exception of the specters, drew a sharp breath.

"And what did you do with that ax?" continued the beautiful prosecutor.

Billy opened one eye. "Hey . . . wait a minute."

And just like that the spell was broken. Billy wasn't quite that dumb, but things might have gone easier for him if he had been.

The prosecutor quickly changed her tactics. The fingers that had caressed Billy's hair suddenly seized it by the handful and shook his big head like a maraca. That's when her appearance began to change. Her lovely skin turned scaly and gray. Her eyes bugged out as big as ping-pong balls, and her ears stretched up, pointy and sharp. Those delicate shoulders stooped. The perfectly straight spine buckled and bent, the backbones popping out like dragon's scales, and the tailbone sprouting into a full-blown tail. The hands, as delicate as doves only seconds before, curled into claws, while the pretty feet twisted into talons.

The Wren sisters screamed and dove beneath their blankets.

"What *is* she?" cried Abigail.

"She appears to be a succubus," said Sam.

"Say what?" I said.

"A succubus," Sam repeated. "A demonic creature that takes the form of a beautiful woman in order to drain the life force of sleeping men."

"Oh," I said.

The succubus hopped up on Billy's chest, her arrow-tipped tail whipping like mad. She breathed foul breath in his face and shrieked at him until he shriveled into a ball. "You little monster! Answer the question! What did you do with that ax? Answer me now!" She pointed a black claw at the dryad, who was gasping like a trout on the bottom of a fisherman's catch basket. "What did you do to this poor creature?"

"Nothing! Nothing!" Billy insisted. "I don't know what you're talking about! I swear! I didn't do it!"

The succubus dug her talons deep into his chest and lashed his face with her claws. "Liar! Liar! You took that ax, whack whack whack, and chopped that tree right to the ground!

Now its spirit lies there dying, and you're a murderer! A murderer!"

With that the chanting began anew.

Billy covered his ears, trying to block out the wave of sound. "No! No! Oh, leave me alone! I didn't do nothing!"

English was never his best subject.

The succubus released him nevertheless, and hopped back to the ground. Billy was left a sobbing, whimpering mess. His tormentor morphed back into the form of a woman and turned to the judge. "I have no further questions for this witness," she said.

Now it was Billy's lawyer's turn. He strode up to the circle of stones and flashed a pearly smile. "There, there, there," he soothed, patting Billy on the shoulder. "I know you're a good boy at heart. You'd never do anything *bad*, now would you?"

"No," Billy sniffed.

"That's right," cooed the handsome lawyer. "You're a *good* boy, aren't you?"

"Yeah," Billy agreed. He was starting to feel more confident, and his talent for telling lies came back to him. "I've always tried to be good. In fact, I don't think I've ever hurt so much as a fly." Now he was just getting cocky.

"That's right. We're going to show the court what a *good* boy we have before us." But this time the handsome lawyer's eye twitched as he pronounced the word good, and the orb bulged ever so slightly.

Billy didn't seem to notice. He only smiled, content to let his lawyer go on singing his praises, while he wallowed in false humility.

But suddenly the man's questions started coming rapid-fire. "You'd never stomp a daisy or tie tin cans to a dog's tail? You'd never throw a firecracker down a rabbit hole or up-root a sapling? You'd never steal eggs from a robin's nest or strip the bark off an elm? You'd never hamstring a jumping frog or pluck the petals off a rose?"

"No, no, no!" Billy answered. "I'd never do any of those things!" But he was starting to sound a little worried. His lawyer's de-meanor had changed.

The man's lustrous skin turned all red, as though something was boiling just beneath the surface. He leaned over Billy, no longer smiling, but still showing his teeth. His eyes were pulsating like strobe lights. "But most important of all," he shouted, "You'd never take a great big ax, whack whack whack, and chop a weeping willow tree down to the ground?"

Billy spoke in the smallest voice I'd ever heard him use. ". . . no."

"Liar! Liar!" roared his lawyer. And almost instantly he morphed into what he truly was. He grew scales and a tail, his hands became claws, his feet talons. He was red, not black, but otherwise he looked a lot like the succubus. "Tell the truth! Tell the truth!" he urged his bewildered client. "You did it! You chopped down that tree and murdered the dryad because it's your nature. You couldn't help yourself. You're a *bad*, bad boy! Change your plea before it's too late. You're guilty. Guilty! GUILTY!"

The crowd instantly took up the chant.

"Hey, wait!" Billy protested. "You're supposed to be on my side." Helplessly, he turned to the judge. "He's supposed to be on *my* side."

"Just as I feared," said Sam. "An incubus. The male counterpart to the succubus."

"Let me guess," I said. "The incubus is a demonic creature who drains the life force of sleeping women."

"Bingo."

"Well, I hope he doesn't quit his night job," Abigail said. "Because he isn't much of a lawyer."

She was right. It was as if the incubus couldn't help himself. I think he really tried his best to defend Billy, but nothing could prevent his true nature from bubbling to the surface. "Admit it!" he thundered. "You chopped that tree down and you're proud of it! You're a mean, rotten, bloody little brat! And you wouldn't have it any other way!"

Billy covered his head with his arms and begged for mercy. He rocked back and forth within the circle of stones, crying and hollering for his mommy. I almost felt sorry for him—almost.

The incubus changed back into his human form and faced the judge. "I have no further questions for this witness."

With a nod from the satyr the two trolls pulled Billy out of the circle of stones and left him whimpering in a pile of wet leaves. Then the satyr said, "Call the next witness."

The succubus stepped forward. She was still in her more appealing womanly form. "The prosecution calls Stacy and Tracy Wren."

Now we all knew what we were doing in a clearing of the forest in the middle of the night. We had been called to testify against Billy-Don't-Do-It, and before the night was through we'd each take our turn in the circle of stones.

The trolls had to carry the Wren sisters up, bed and all. The rest of us were left sitting on the cold ground. The girls clung to each other, their teeth chattering from fear or the cold or both. It didn't take long for the succubus to show them her uglier side. She railed at them, her forked tongue flickering, her scales squirming with rage. She demanded they tell the court what they'd witnessed in the clearing on that fateful afternoon.

139

But to everyone's surprise the Wren sisters didn't make for good witnesses. "I don't remember," insisted Stacy. "The sun was in my eyes," claimed Tracy.

I knew they weren't being truthful, and I didn't understand why they of all people would take up for Billy-Don't-Do-It. He'd been so mean to them.

The succubus menaced the Wrens with every scare tactic in her repertoire, yet the girls refused to betray the kid they had hated most of their lives. Ultimately, she had to give up. "I have no more questions for these . . . witnesses," she told the satyr.

Then it was Sam Simon's turn. The prosecutor took a different tack with him. She stood before him in her loveliest shape and ran a perfectly manicured fingernail down his cheek and under his chin. "You'll tell me the truth, now, won't you, Sammy?"

Sam was a bright kid and I'm sure he knew well enough to take any sweet nothings this sinister siren whispered with a grain of salt. But that succubus could sound awfully nice when she wanted to. It got to the point where Sam's glasses started to fog up a little. He took them off and wiped them on his shirt.

"So did you see it, Sammy-Whammy?" the succubus pressed ever so sweetly. "Did you see what happened to the weeping willow tree?"

It looked like she was going to prove too much for old Sam. It looked like he was going to break down and tell her everything she wanted to know. After all, he owed Billy for a hundred wedgies, a thousand Indian burns, and about a million nuggies. Why not pay it all back with interest?

"I didn't see anything that day," Sam said at last. "I didn't see anything at all. I wasn't wearing my glasses." He held the spectacles up as if they were exhibit A.

Now I'd known Sam since he could walk, and never once saw him without those glasses. He even swam with them strapped around his head.

The prosecutor was disappointed. She put on a brave face, but you could see she was itching to revert back to demon mode and take a bite out of Sam's neck. "I have no further questions for this witness," she told the judge.

They called Abigail up next. This time the succubus didn't even pretend. She changed just as quick as you can flip a light switch and came at the new witness with every trick in the devil's play book. She danced in the air and drew flaming shapes with her claws. She disappeared in a poof of smoke and reappeared behind Abigail, in front of Abigail, on top of Abigail's shoulders. "What did you see? What did you see?" she hissed. Finally she split herself into three and surrounded Abigail, joining

141

hands with her other selves and dancing ring-around-the-rosy around the circle of stones. "Tell the court how Billy-Don't-Do-It chopped down the weeping willow tree!" she demanded.

Abigail calmly cleared her throat. I was amazed at her poise. She looked at the dying dryad, and everyone could tell she felt very sorry to see the creature suffering so.

That does it, I thought. *Billy's done for.*

"I'm afraid I didn't really see anything that day," Abigail said. "I was the last one in the clearing, and it was all over by the time I got there."

I couldn't believe my ears. Abigail hated Billy more than any of us. It seemed that everyone was so afraid of what the dark creatures would do with Billy-Don't-Do-It they were actually sticking up for him.

As for Billy, he was lounging in the leaves with his hands behind his head, looking quite relieved. I watched him, astounded that he was going to get away with it all, the way he always did. And the next thing I knew the trolls had a hold of me. They dragged me up to the circle of stones. I'd been so distracted I hadn't even heard them call my name.

"Thomas Grey," the prosecutor sang. She was in her absolute loveliest form. "What did you see on the afternoon in question? I just know you'll tell me what I want to know, Tommy. You're such a nice, handsome boy."

I took a big gulp. My palms were sweaty. I knew she was a demon, but boy she was pretty—when she wanted to be.

I glanced over at Billy. He was watching me closely. I held his fate in my hands and he knew it. But still he couldn't help himself. He had to smile that mean little smile. He figured he had nothing to fear from me.

"I saw everything," I told the court. "He's guilty. He did it. He took his Dad's ax, whack whack whack, and chopped down the weeping willow tree."

The forest exploded with a thousand bloodthirsty exclamations. The creatures of the night chanted themselves hoarse. "Guilty. Guilty! GUILTY!" was the cry from every fanged mouth and twisted beak.

Billy looked at me like I had just punched him in the stomach, which is probably what I should have done a long time ago. He turned to his lawyer and tried desperately to get the incubus to cross-examine me. However, the handsome demon was too busy examining himself in a hand mirror, primping his golden locks.

My friends stared wide-eyed from atop the Wren sisters' bed. They couldn't believe I'd surrendered Billy to the whim of this macabre court. But I had. And I'm still not sure why. I'd like to think the succubus clouded my mind, as it was certainly in her

power to do, but that simply wasn't the case. I'd like to think that none of it matters anyway, because it was all a dream. But it wasn't a dream. It was real.

"SILENCE!" the satyr roared.

Gradually the noise subsided.

The satyr spoke again. "Billy-Don't-Do-It, your own friend has testified that you chopped down the weeping willow tree, thus killing the dryad who resided within."

As if to prove the satyr's point, the withered dryad took a last lingering gasp and stirred no more.

"This court finds you guilty," the satyr pronounced. "Guilty of murder most base. Guilty of murder for murder's sake."

"GUILTY! GUILTY! GUILTY!" The sound seemed to emanate not only from the creatures in the clearing, but from every tree in the forest.

"Now it is the decision of this court," the judge continued, "that the human boy known as Billy-Don't-Do-It be handed over to the justice of the dryad race. May they do with him as they see fit!"

"No!" Billy pleaded.

But it was too late. The horn blew one last time.

The trees began to stir. The branches shaking, the leaves trembling. It was as if a gale was sweeping through the forest or an earthquake erupting below, but neither was the case. Long, stick-like limbs began to shoot up from the soil, like the legs of giant praying mantis. They pulled themselves to the surface, their knobby joints creaking. They stared at Billy with their knothole eyes. They frowned at him with their jagged mouths. Then all at once they reached for him, engulfing his small figure in a nest of creepers and vines.

"No!" he screamed. "Help! Please! Someone!" But no one could help him now.

It looked as though he had fallen asleep on the very spot a hundred years ago, and just now woke to find the forest grown over him. The dryads began to sink back beneath their trees. And down they dragged Billy-Don't-Do-It. Beneath the forest floor and beneath all the helpless or inanimate creatures—the flora and the fauna—that he hated so much. The leaves closed over his head like the waves over a sinking ship.

My four friends and I never spoke of that night. They never asked me why I'd testified against Billy. Sam didn't ask. Even Abigail didn't ask. We went to our houses in silence. I guess the harpies flew us all back on top of the Wren sisters' bed. I don't really remember.

One thing I know for certain is this. From that night on, whenever a neighborhood kid was up to no good—I mean whenever someone was about to do something really nasty, like pick on a little kid or chuck a bag of kittens into the lake—we always knew how to

stop him. We didn't say, "Knock it off, Joe," or "Quit it, Jimmy." No matter what the kid's name happened to be, all we ever had to say was, "Billy-Don't-Do-It!" That stopped the meanest little buggers dead in their tracks.

Those kids might not have been in the forest the night of Billy's trial. But then . . . they *might* have been. It could have easily have been any one of them. And that was all they needed to know.

NINE

Witch-Baby

The trouble started when Gretchen saw the thing in the woods. She claimed it stood no higher than three feet. She called it Witch-Baby and said its eyes looked like they were on fire.

That was the year the Whittaker family farm fell on hard times. The animals grew sickly and scrawny. The crops withered and died. Soon all the tools were rusty and the tractor was left abandoned on the back forty. Even the harrow, that steel toothed monster of a machine, sat idle on the side of the cornfield.

The harrow had terrified Lloyd Whittaker and his sister Bess ever since they were toddlers. It consisted of a big engine and two small wheels in back, with a bucket seat and a few levers on top. In the front, two larger wheels were stuck like the eyes of a shark on the opposite sides of the gaping mouth. And

what a mouth it was—eight feet across and cram-packed with glittering teeth. When the engine rumbled to life and the wheels began to turn, these teeth would rend the hard earth, churning up rocks and digging long furrows in which corn could be planted.

But no new corn could be planted when the old corn was too rotten to harvest. So the harrow hibernated in the weeds, grinning in hungry silence.

There was a hungry silence in the house as well, where the Whittakers—Ma, Pa, Lloyd, and Bess—all found themselves trapped in a constant state of misery. They were held hostage by a tyrant, a holy terror who broke the silence with wild outbursts and rampaging attacks of temper. She smashed dishes and upended chairs, she kicked shins and bit fingers, all without the slightest provocation. She stamped her feet and flew into wild tantrums whenever she didn't get her way.

She was Gretchen Whittaker, four years old, and the baby of the family.

Lloyd simply couldn't understand why his parents didn't punish his little sister. He was thirteen, and Bess was eleven and three-quarters, but they both knew they would never have gotten away with the terrible things Gretchen did every day. "Why don't they spank her, or make her sit in the corner, or *something*?" he complained to Bess.

"Because she's the baby," Bess said. "Ma doesn't have the heart to punish her. Neither does Pa."

"She ain't a baby," Lloyd insisted. "She walks and talks and kicks like an old mule. And when I was four, I didn't kick anybody, or else I would have gotten my hide tanned."

But Ma and Pa simply couldn't bring themselves to discipline their youngest child, no matter how badly she misbehaved. "It's just a phase," Ma would say. "She'll grow out of it."

And Pa would shut his eyes and nod his head in agreement.

But of all the things his baby sister did, what made Lloyd maddest of all wasn't the kicking, biting, or tantrum throwing. What really made him see red was the excuse Gretchen always gave for her outrageous antics. She could be caught standing over the shattered pieces of a lamp, or found hiding in the closet after bruising an innocent shin, and she would smile and say: "It wasn't me. The Witch-Baby did it."

Lloyd would sigh in exasperation and cry, "For the last time, there is no such thing as a Witch-Baby!"

But his little sister would only giggle and run away.

Things went on this way for many months. Gretchen's behavior didn't improve. In fact, it seemed to grow much worse, as far as her brother was concerned. Lloyd returned home

from school one afternoon and found his room in complete disarray. Someone had committed the capital crime of messing with his stuff. His baseball cards were strewn all about the floor, his trophies were knocked from their shelf (some of them broken), and one of his model airplanes was dashed into a thousand plastic pieces.

Lloyd ran down to the kitchen, shouting for his mother as he went. He found Bess sitting at the kitchen table, eating a slice of stale bread. "Where's Ma?" he demanded, barely able to control his temper.

"She went to the market to see what ten dollars would buy," Bess explained.

"Where's Pa?"

"He went with her. They took the truck. They said to tell you you're in charge 'til they get back."

"I'm in charge?"

"Yeah, but don't get a swelled head over it. They'll be back in an hour."

Lloyd stormed out of the kitchen and stomped up the stairs. "I'm in charge," he repeated. *"I'm* in charge." He marched straight to Gretchen's room and banged on the door.

"Who is it?" Gretchen sang from within.

"You know who it is!" he thundered, shoving his way inside.

She was sitting Indian-style in the middle of her bed and plucking all the hair from the head of a naked doll.

"You had no right to mess with my stuff," Lloyd shouted, wagging a finger at her. "You had better keep out of my room, Gretchen. Or you're gonna be in big trouble."

"I wasn't in your old room," she pouted. Then she smiled that wicked little smile. "It was the Witch-Baby. The Witch-Baby did it."

If Lloyd had been angry before, this denial sent him into a blind fury. "YOU LITTLE LIAR!" he raged. "You did it! You broke my stuff! Not the Witch-Baby! There is no Witch-Baby. You made that up."

"No, I didn't," sang Gretchen.

"Yes, you did! Yes, you did! And I'll prove it too!"

By now Bess had come to see what all the shouting was about. She found her brother stomping around the little room and waving his arms like a madman. "What's going on?" she asked.

"She says the Witch-Baby was the one who trashed my room," Lloyd explained. "Because we all know it couldn't have been Gretchen. She'd never do anything like that. So it must've been the famous Witch-Baby."

"Gretchen!" Bess scolded. "What have you done now?"

"No, no, it was the Witch-Baby," Lloyd persisted. "It's to blame, whatever it is. But I just want to know one thing. Where is this

Witch-Baby, Gretchen?" He knelt down and gazed into her eyes. "Show it to me? Where does it live?"

"She lives in there," Gretchen said, pointing to the closet. "But she's not there now. She's out in the field ruining the crops."

"How convenient," Lloyd said and stepped over to the closet. The door was made from solid oak and held up with iron hinges.

"Be careful," Bess urged.

"Oh, give me a break," Lloyd said and pulled the door open.

Inside there were some dresses and coats hanging on hangers, with a few pairs of little shoes on the floor. There was also a strong smell of mothballs, but nothing out of the ordinary.

"So this is where she lives, huh," Lloyd said sarcastically. "And what does she eat? Mothballs?"

"She doesn't live *there*, silly," Gretchen said.

"You just said she does."

"No," the child insisted. "Behind the clothes."

Lloyd looked at Bess and sighed. Then he parted the dresses and coats and revealed something a little strange. Something that gave him pause.

It was a second door very similar to the first, except it was only a third as big. Neither Lloyd nor Bess had ever seen this funny little door before, but then they'd never had cause to look inside their sister's closet. They exchanged a curious glance and shrugged their shoulders. Then Lloyd reached down and turned the rusty knob.

The miniature door swung inward to reveal a dark and damp space—a small room behind the closet from which an awful stench began to emanate.

"Oh, man!" Bess cried. "What's that awful smell? It's like something died in there."

That's when they heard the buzzing. The sound was faint at first, but it was definitely coming from inside the small room.

"I'd better take a look," Lloyd said.

"Oh, please don't," Bess begged.

But her brother was determined to get to the bottom of the matter. He knelt down and stuck his head through the small door. At first he didn't see anything, but then he noticed a bunch of dead grass gathered up into some kind of nest, and he realized he was inside a den. A den that belonged to something very real—something Gretchen referred to as the Witch-Baby. The stench was overwhelming.

Suddenly the buzzing grew much louder, and Lloyd saw what was making the sound. Hundreds upon hundreds of flies came pouring out of the darkness and swarmed straight

for his face. He jumped back, spitting and slapping himself to get the filthy insects away.

Bess screamed as the flies buzzed all around the room. They lit upon the floor, the furniture, the walls, and the ceiling. They even got in her hair, and she did a wild dance out into the hall, shaking and slapping like mad. Lloyd wasn't far behind.

"The Witch-Baby won't like you messing round in her room," Gretchen hissed, still sitting on the bed. The flies buzzed about her like a dirty cloud, but she didn't seem to mind. "She's gonna get you now. Better run and hide."

The flies chased Lloyd and Bess all the way downstairs. They beat feet across the porch and out into the farmyard, bound for the water trough. They sloshed about, trying to clean their faces and all the places where the insects had touched their skin. Then they both began to feel very strange, as though they were being watched by something malevolent, and their splashing abruptly ended.

"Did you see that?" Lloyd asked.

"See what?" Bess replied, glancing all about.

"Out in the cornfield," her brother said, pointing straight ahead.

The dried stalks were swaying slightly in the breeze. There wasn't a sound—not so much as a chirping cicada.

"I don't see anything," said Bess.

But then she did see something. There was a fluttering among the corn stalks and a small but sinister shape zigzagged across the field, giggling and singing to itself in a strange sort of way.

"It was watching us," Lloyd said. "I saw its eyes. They were like fire."

And to Bess' great surprise he plunged into the cornfield and made after the mysterious thing like a hound dog on the trail of a raccoon. Then she surprised herself when she went running after him. At first she lost him completely and was alone in the forest of wilted brown husks. She was about to panic when she was grabbed by the wrist and pulled to the ground.

Lloyd squatted next to her, his index finger pressed to his lips. He pointed and whispered, "Over there."

Bess looked and squinted, shielded her eyes and bobbed her head. Far off between the rows of dead corn something was stirring. Lloyd had found a stick and he used it to part the dry husks as they crept forward. They came to within a few yards of the spot, and he whispered again.

"Okay. On three. Ready?"

"Ready?" Bess repeated skeptically. "Ready for what?"

Lloyd sighed. "We're gonna rush her! It! Whatever!"

"You're joking."

"No," he insisted. "I'm gonna get to the bottom of this one way or another. Now are you with me or not?"

"Fine," his sister said, summoning her courage. "Let's get it over with."

Lloyd took a few steps forward. "Now!"

They went crashing between the cornstalks, Lloyd swinging the stick like a snakebeater and Bess whooping and hollering as if the whole world were on fire. They thrashed up a mess of dead husks, and soon realized there was nothing there. No evil creature. No Witch-Baby. Not so much as a milk snake.

But there had been something there. They'd seen it. They'd felt it watching them. They looked at one another and shrugged in mutual frustration.

Then they heard a buzzing sound.

"Oh, no!" Bess said. "I can't take any more flies."

Lloyd held up his hand. "No, that's not a swarm of flies."

The sound grew louder and the ground started to shake.

"I've heard this before," Bess said, trying hard to remember.

"RUN!" her brother shouted and grabbed her by the arm.

Behind them a dozen cornstalks vanished beneath a row of grinding metal teeth. The harrow had rumbled up out of nowhere—the buzzing sound had been that of its engine— and now it was headed straight toward them. The seat at the top was empty and the levers seemed to move all on their own.

Lloyd and Bess darted to the left, but the monstrous contraption only followed, pulverizing the soil and rending the hard ground as if it wanted to rip the earth right out from beneath their feet.

"Run faster!" Lloyd bellowed.

"I'm trying!" Bess said, panting for breath.

The harrow roared like a beast, its engine snorting smoke and its grinning mouth eating up everything that lay in its path. The big teeth spun and gouged the ground, spewing dirt, rocks, and rotten corn in all directions.

Lloyd and Bess burst from the field like frightened crows and tried to cut across the farmyard. They didn't get far before Bess tripped and fell. It wasn't a stick or a stone that she'd stumbled over, however, but something unseen, small and very strong. In fact it felt as though two little hands had hooked her ankle and pulled her to the ground.

Now she lay there helpless, with the harrow barreling down upon her. Lloyd wheeled around and helped her to her feet, but the machine was right behind them. And it seemed to be gaining speed. Bess could only hobble now, as her ankle had turned, and Lloyd had to support her. They were only thirty yards

from their own front porch, but neither of them believed they would make it.

Suddenly there was a great storm of dust out on the road, and something big and shiny came barreling onto the Whittaker farm. Lloyd saw a streak of red and realized it was the truck. Ma and Pa were back from the market. Pa gunned it and crashed into the harrow at no less than forty miles an hour.

The big machine groaned like a wounded woolly mammoth and was flipped upside down. The metal teeth spun in the air and smoke belched from the engine in sputtering puffs.

The truck sat idling, with the dust settling around it and the radiator hissing steam. The front fender was badly dented, but the old Chevy was otherwise unscathed. Ma and Pa opened the doors and clambered out. Ma rushed over to check on her children, hugging them in turn, then hugging them both at the same time. Pa removed his hat and scratched his head, studying the harrow as though it was a flying saucer that had just crash-landed in the farmyard.

Later he would chalk it up to a case of bad wiring. But Lloyd and Bess knew better. Something far more sinister than bad wiring had caused the harrow to go haywire. They tried to tell their parents what they'd seen and heard, but it was all very difficult to explain.

"You have to see that little room behind Gretchen's closet," Lloyd urged. "It's horrible!"

But Ma and Pa Whittaker only shook their heads. "Your great-grandfather built this house," Pa said. "There are no little rooms, not behind Gretchen's closet or any of the others."

"But the Witch-Baby is real!" Bess insisted. "She tried to kill us after Lloyd found her den."

"Young lady," Ma began. "That is patent nonsense. Your sister is simply going through a phase. She'll grow out of it, sure enough."

And just as her mother spoke, Gretchen came scampering down the stairs, giggling and singing some nonsensical song. She glared at Lloyd as she passed, and suddenly he felt something bite him on the shin.

"Ouch!" he cried, rubbing the wound, which had begun to bleed.

Then he was bitten again, on the hand this time, and once more, just above the knee. He hopped about in great pain, while his mother begged him to tell her what was the matter.

"Don't you see? Don't you see?" Bess hollered. "It's the Witch-Baby. She's out to get him."

Soon the entire house was a tumult, with Lloyd crying out in pain and Gretchen running amuck, her feet always kicking and her

159

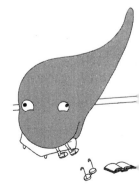

hands forever slapping. She cackled like a wild child and talked constantly with her friend the Witch-Baby. She sang her little songs and danced among the debris of shattered lamps and broken dishes. And another voice—very much like her own—would answer back from the darkened corners of the house.

"Did you hear that?" Bess demanded of her parents, each time she heard a voice that didn't seem to belong to her sister.

But Ma and Pa only shook their heads and looked puzzled.

The upheaval continued for several days. On the third day Lloyd came down with a fever and took to his bed. He muttered in his sleep, tossing and turning and kicking the blankets to the floor. When he woke he was delirious and mumbled something about seeing the Witch-Baby in his dreams. She had crept out from behind the door, her terrible eyes aglow, and her body shriveled and small, like a rotted apple core. She had extended her claws and reached for his throat.

"It was just a dream," his mother soothed, mopping his forehead with a cool cloth.

But Ma's best efforts at doctoring her son were thwarted when Gretchen flew into the room and pounced upon the bed. She jumped up and down and laughed like a demented little fiend, jostling her poor brother and worsening his condition. And just like her singing, the laughter was echoed by something that seemed, at least to Lloyd, to be everywhere at once. It came up from under the bed, down from the rafters, and out of the closet—a cruel cackle, devoid of any real mirth.

Lloyd moaned and rolled over, trying to avoid his sister's stomping feet. Ma looked down at him suffering so, and she simply couldn't stand it any longer. "THAT IS ENOUGH!" she shouted, her own voice reaching the rafters and silencing the laughter. Then she caught Gretchen in midair and pulled the girl down off the bed.

Gretchen squiggled and squirmed, trying to free herself from her mother's grasp, but Mrs. Whittaker was bound and determined. She carried the little girl downstairs and sat her in a chair in a corner of the kitchen. "Child," she scolded. "You are going to stop all this misbehavin'. You are going to mind your Pa and me. You are going to be nice to your sister, and you are going to leave your brother be."

Gretchen's mouth was agape, her eyes wide with surprise.

Pa and Bess peered around the corner, their own mouths agape.

"Now you can sit in that chair," Ma continued, "and think about what a bad little girl you've been. And Witch-Baby or no Witch-Baby, you will learn to behave."

There was a long silence, and it looked as though Gretchen might cry. Her little lip

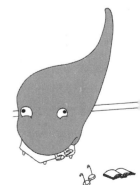

quivered and she took a deep breath. But then in a very small voice she said two little words: "Yes, ma'am."

Lloyd's fever broke the next morning. Soon his strength returned and he was up on his feet. This was especially good news, as it wasn't long before there were to chores be done. The crops grew healthy again and the animals all recovered, feeding and getting fat. It wasn't long before the corn needed picking and the cows wanted milking.

Gretchen changed too. She was made to sit up straight and mind what she was told. Ma and Pa started to raise her the same way they'd raised Lloyd and Bess, and she became the sweet and sunny child she was always meant to be.

As for the Witch-Baby, Lloyd and Bess didn't see her much anymore—neither did Gretchen. Once in a while they might hear her singing a sad song from up in the rafters or scrabbling about inside the walls. But the sounds faded as the years went by and eventually the Whittaker farm seemed entirely free of her presence.

Still, Lloyd never forgot the terrible ordeal. And occasionally—perhaps once a year—when Gretchen was angry, he might just catch her shift her eyes and whisper something as though she were speaking to an invisible friend. Then the wind would blow, bringing the faintest echo of a reply: a bit of singing, perhaps, or a little cackle, cruel and without the slightest hint of mirth.

TEN

The Parade of Night

My sister and I always figured our hometown was just about the dullest place on the planet. There was simply nothing to do in Millsap Hollow. There were a few hundred houses, with white picket fences and manicured lawns. And little else. The nearest mall was miles away—much too far to get there on your bike.

Sometimes it seemed like the only thing that made Millsap any different from a million other small towns was the creepy old cemetery. It was in the middle of town, up on a hill, with a big brick wall around it like a medieval fort. Most people preferred to pretend the place didn't even exist. And I didn't have much interest in a bunch of moldy old headstones myself, but my morbid sister liked to hang out there.

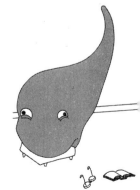

Penelope was a weird kid. She dressed all in black like she thought she was in a horror movie or something.

That's why it nearly killed her when they canceled Halloween.

At school they told us not to come in costume, eat too much candy, or do anything deemed as "too scary." Then we were told that the mayor had called off all Halloween related activities, including costume parties and trick-or-treating. Apparently a small but pushy group of parents didn't like the idea of a bunch of kids parading through the streets in all sorts of inappropriate costumes. They decided to call the day "Harvest Fest" instead of Halloween, and everywhere we looked we saw displays of corn and uncarved pumpkins. We were supposed to dress in flannels and blue jeans and go on hayrides in the school parking lot.

"This is unbelievable," Penelope said as we wandered the school grounds, dodging the teachers who were dressed in suspenders and straw hats. "Halloween is all we have to look forward to in this town. Now we can't even go trick-or-treating?" Everyone else was wearing flannel like they'd been told, but she was dressed in her usual black sweater, black slacks, black shoes, and black jacket.

"I just hope they don't serve corn at lunch," I said. "I've seen enough corn to last me a lifetime." I was still itching from the hayride.

The first cold wind of the season came whistling down on us and suddenly the air was filled with black leaflets. They swirled round in the sky and slowly spiraled down like earthbound ravens. The school custodian, the teachers, and even our principal started scooping them up at once. They tore them to shreds and shoved them into trash cans. But Penelope managed to get ahold of one, as there were so many it was impossible to confiscate them all.

She held it up. It read:

Come one, come all! See the Parade of Night! Join Drum Major Leviticus Lazarus Maelstrom and his Band of Beasts and Bugaboos. Raise your heart! Raise your spirits! Raise the dead! Tonight and tonight only!

I figured it had to be some kind of gag. And I certainly didn't want any part of it. Needless to say my sister saw things differently. Her face positively lit up when she read the leaflet. "Band of Beasts and Bugaboos," she said, with a sense of wonder. "That sounds pretty cool."

"Oh, no," I said. "Oh, no, no, no."

My sister ignored me. "We have got to check this out," she proclaimed.

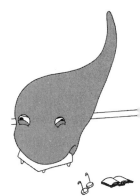

"You can't be serious," I said. "It sounds like a real freak show to me. Besides, we don't even know when or where it's gonna start."

As I spoke another leaflet came fluttering down. It read: *10 o'clock. Custard Street.*

"That's our street!" Penelope cried.

"Forget it," I told her. "I'm not even leaving the house."

She glared at me angrily.

"Look, Jon," she began, "there's no way I'm missing this parade. You're the one who always says how boring this town is. Now's our one chance for some excitement."

"Fine," I told her. "You go ahead and join the freak show. You're so weird you'll probably fit right in." I walked away and left her holding the black leaflet.

"See if I don't, you big wuss!" she shouted after me.

At home she spent the entire evening staring out the living room window. Every time I went into the living room she tried to goad me into going to see the parade with her. I did my level best to ignore her. Finally, she lowered the boom. "Okay. Fine. Be that way," she said. "Let your little sister go out by herself on Halloween night. If I don't come back you can just tell Mom and Dad I was too weird to worry about."

"Look, Penelope," I said. "I think you're setting yourself up for a big disappointment. You don't even know if this parade is gonna come off, let alone be any good. The whole thing might be some kind of practical joke."

"Oh, I don't think so," she replied.

"What makes you say that?" I had a sinking feeling in the pit of my stomach.

Penelope was gazing fixedly out the window. "Because the parade is about to start," she said.

I went and joined her at the window. The sky had turned violet with the onset of evening, and four strange figures were advancing up the street with military precision. They avoided the street lamps that had been lit to combat the encroaching dark. Then they came to a halt, one, two, three, four on the sidewalk in front of our house.

They all wore black uniforms with big brass buttons and tall hats. But there was something very unusual about these fellows. In fact none of them appeared to be quite human. The first figure was dressed as a drum major. He looked positively ghoulish, with shriveled blue skin and tiny pink eyes. He had a big forehead and a lantern jaw. The black uniform hung from his gaunt frame and the big fuzzy hat sat perched jauntily atop his scabby head. He also held a baton that looked very much like a human femur. This had to be

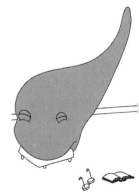

Leviticus Lazarus Maelstrom, Drum Major of the Band of Beasts and Bugaboos.

Further evidence of this came in the form of the figure that stood directly behind Mr. Maelstrom. This fellow wore a bass drum strapped around his shoulders. He also happened to be half hyena and half man. That is to say that he stood on two legs like a man, but otherwise looked very much like a hyena. He had a long, whiskery snout and two pointy ears stuck up on either side of his hat. And every part of him that wasn't covered by the strange uniform was covered instead by a mottled brown and white fur. He clutched a drumstick in his claw-like hand and rolled his yellow eyes back in his head.

Next in line was a trumpet player who was also a goat-man. His hat was pushed back in order to leave room for the two crooked horns that grew out of his head. He had dirty white fur and a pointed beard hung below his black muzzle. He crinkled his nose up in an ugly way and pawed at the ground with his cloven foot.

The fourth member of the little procession was a tuba player, who appeared to be some sort of boar-man. His bloated pink body was stuffed into the uniform, and a pair of tusks jutted out from beneath his snout, which was slimy with snot. His bulging eyes darted wildly from side to side, as he sniffed at the air and snorted once or twice.

I turned to say something to Penelope and discovered that she was already heading for the door. "They've come to take us away, he-he, ha-ha," she called over her shoulder.

I had no choice but to run after her.

We crossed the yard and approached the four of them. The hyena-man was already casting me sidelong glances, grinning and showing his pointy teeth. I didn't care for that in the least.

Mr. Maelstrom raised his baton. The hyena-man pounded his drum. Once. Twice. Three times.

And suddenly a whole army of strange creatures came crawling out of the gloom. *We've seen the beasts*, I thought. *Now these must be the bugaboos.* There were wood sprites and trolls, changelings and all sorts of things you read about if you read the wrong sort of books. There were incubi and succubi, and I swore I even saw a doppelganger that looked just like me. He darted in and out of the crowd, peeking out from behind the other figures, grinning and winking at me.

There were more traditional Halloween types too. A contingent of haughty vampires hung on the fringes of the crowd. They studied everyone with their hypnotic eyes, their white skin practically glowing and their capes fluttering in the breeze. Nearby, a coven of witches stood in a semicircle, whispering and

speaking in strange tongues. One of them nodded and smiled at Penelope, and Penelope smiled right back.

I guess the whole lot was assembled now, because Leviticus Lazarus Maelstrom waved his baton in a wide arch, and the hyena-man began to beat his drum again.

The bizarre crowd formed itself into a kind of disorganized procession, and off we went, marching in lock step. Penelope and I marched right alongside the others, because we simply couldn't do otherwise. There was something in the way that hyena pounded the drum. Rhythmic. Hypnotic. We fell into a kind of trance.

Soon the goat-man joined in on the trumpet and the boar-man sounded his tuba. The notes burst forth mellow and fat. It was a strange sort of tune. It gave you a kind of dread deep in the pit of your stomach and made you feel like you were headed toward something unspeakable—something you never wanted to see. Yet the otherworldly noises, the rhythm and the beat, compelled us to keep moving our feet.

On we went, up toward the center of town.

"Oh, great," I said, quite sarcastically. "I think I know where we're headed."

But if Penelope heard, she chose to ignore me.

The hyena-man was still watching me, his eyes lolling, his tongue wagging. He seemed to be dreaming up some bloody red scheme. He pounded the drum, pounded the drum. And the goat-man's trumpet went blat-blat-blat.

We crested a hill and there stood the cemetery. The brick wall only reminded me that I wasn't supposed to go where I didn't even want to go.

But all around that wall stood an assemblage the likes of which Millsap Hollow had never seen. There was a score of creatures standing in wait around the gate. There were more beast-men who wore the same black uniforms with shiny gold buttons and towering hats. There were other things too—freaky things that could only be described as indescribable. And there were more instruments: bassoons, oboes, clarinets, saxophones, sousaphones, and trombones. Not to mention the drums—drums of all sizes. And cymbals too—clutched in the claws of a particularly demented hyena-man, who looked as though he couldn't wait to crash them, over and over, until our eardrums bled.

But for the time being all the instruments were silent. We had come to a halt, and now stood among the unholy host at the gates of the cemetery. My good friend Mr. Hyena stood right behind me. His hot breath hit the back of my neck.

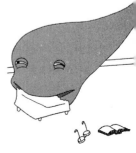

The things around us seemed impatient. The beast-men panted and pawed at the ground, their eyes shining in the moonlight. The vampires drummed their lithe fingers, while the forest creatures twittered about like kids on Christmas morning. The witches waited in serene silence.

My doppelganger sidled up to me and cleared his throat. "Say, Jon," he whispered in my own voice. "If you don't feel like going to school tomorrow I'd love to take your place."

"Get out of here," I hissed and raised my fist.

He dodged back into the crowd.

Then I looked up and saw a figure standing atop the wall like some great bird of prey. I tapped Penelope on the shoulder and pointed. It was Maelstrom. How he'd popped up there so quickly, we hadn't a clue. He raised his bone baton and began to wave it with all the ceremony of a choir conductor.

Instantly the band of beast men raised their instruments, and a screeching, wailing cacophony rose into the night. The drums were like terrible thunder. The pounding, driving beat shook the ground. It also shook your legs, and rose up into your stomach, leaving you feeling all funny inside.

Maelstrom waved his baton some more, and the horns and woodwinds were reined in a bit. The music became less chaotic. Except for the hyena with the cymbals. There was no controlling him. He smashed and bashed with maniacal delight, his tongue flopping and flinging saliva in every direction.

But the horns were melodious and strong, and the woodwinds soft and bittersweet. I fought the urge to surrender myself to the tune. I didn't want to be carried away toward that awful thing, whatever it was.

Yet the drums got me in the end. Bum-bum-bum, up though the legs and into the stomach. And suddenly I had to pick up my feet. We marched among the beasts and bugaboos, Penelope smiling and laughing. "They're taking us away, he-he, ha-ha."

She fit right in, just as I knew she would.

We went through the gates and straight into the cemetery. We rolled up the path like a tidal wave of noise. The flowers on the graves wilted at the sound of the music; the blades of grass curled up like the legs of dead spiders.

On we marched, weaving among the head-stones and trampling the flowers. The heavy notes burst from the horns more quickly now, and the drums pounded even faster. Our hearts were thumping, keeping time with the beat.

Then I saw what it was I'd been dreading—that thing no one wanted to see.

It started with a thousand shriveled hands grasping and clawing their way out of the

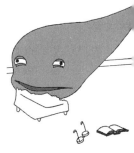

graves. Then up rose the bodies, wiggling and squirming out of the ground like worms after a rainstorm.

Most of them had been dead for years and were nothing more than skeletons. Their hollow eye sockets and ghastly grinning teeth were horrible to see. Their rib cages were empty and exposed, all the organs having wasted away.

Others had died more recently. These were the worst. They still had bugs on them, and their rotting skin was all splotchy and gray. Their clothes were like ribbons, and they were putrid with decay.

The things who'd brought us were bad enough, wild, scary, and unpredictable. But there was something far worse about this uprising of the dead. Maybe it was how they'd always been there, right in the middle of town. And we knew they were there, silently waiting for us to join them, no matter how hard we tried to forget.

Leviticus Lazarus Maelstrom, still standing atop the wall, waved his baton in a new way. Instantly, the music changed— the melody became more methodic, the beat more regular.

Before I knew what was happening, we were marching again. We went straight out of the cemetery and into the center of town, with one thousand dead people in tow. They shuffled and jerked and twitched, ambling their way along down the middle of the street.

The beast men stomped along in front, their instruments and their eyes gleaming in the moonlight. Penelope and I were still among them, although I tried to distance myself from the hyenas, and kept an eye out for my doppelganger.

As we progressed, I noticed that scores of the dead were wandering away. They climbed over the white picket fences and tread upon the manicured lawns. They walked right up to the houses and began knocking on the doors and pecking at the windows.

"Let us in. Let us in," they called to the people inside, their voices hollow. "We've come home. Let us in."

People locked their doors and windows, and huddled in closets and basements. But the dead were persistent. They swarmed around the houses like a plague of locusts. "We've come home. Let us in. Let us in."

The people were terror-stricken. They ran out of their homes and into the street—whole families fleeing from that ghastly parade of night.

Yet the procession marched on and the band played on. A large throng of the dead still shuffled along around us. Penelope was laughing with the hyena-men, the shrill cackles rising above the pounding of the drums.

Soon we trudged on to the school grounds of Millsap Middle. Several people had holed

up in the gym there. They'd barred the doors and boarded up the windows.

The parade came to a halt in front of the building. The legions of dead began to pound on the doors and claw at the walls. "Let us in. Let us in."

"Go away!" shouted the people inside. "Go back to the cemetery where you belong."

Then Leviticus Lazarus Maelstrom went gliding up between the rows of beast men and the ranks of bugaboos. He raised his hand and the gym doors flew open.

We all swept in behind him—Penelope and me, the scary, the hairy, and the thronging dead. We were truly an awful sight to behold. The people inside were armed with gardening tools and torches. The mayor stepped forward, brandishing a shotgun.

"Stay back," he cried. "Stay back, I tell you!"

But the dead lurched forward, the witches urging them on.

The people raised their shovels, rakes, and hoes. The mayor cocked his shotgun.

I pulled Penelope to the side, and ducked down. This was going to be ugly.

But nothing happened. No one moved. There wasn't a sound. Even the music had died away.

Mr. Maelstrom stood in the middle of the parquet floor, with the living in front of him and the dead right behind. "Ahem, ahem," he said, clearing his throat and smiling his jack-o-lantern smile. "Ladies and gentleman, what is it you plan to do with your pruning shears and weed-eaters? Kill what is already dead?"

"Why did you bring them here?" the mayor demanded. "They don't belong here. They belong in the cemetery—in their graves."

Maelstrom doffed his high hat and picked at a scab on his head. "My good sir," he said. "You are mistaken. This is precisely where they belong. For you see, they built this gymnasium, this school, and this town. They paved the streets and put up the houses. They wrote the books you read and made the laws you obey—or maybe disobey.

"They're your grandparents, and great-grandparents, and great-great—well, you get the idea. Yet you give them not a moment's thought. You cancel their night—their one meager night—their All Hallow's Eve. But, try as you might, you can't escape them. They're here, a bigger part of your lives than you dare admit, and they will remain with you forevermore."

At that Leviticus Lazarus Maelstrom returned his hat to his head, and led his band of

beast men and bugaboos out of the gym. The instruments were playing again, but the music was softer now. The hyena-man poked me in the ribs with his drumstick and gave me a wink. Then all the hyenas started to cackle. And the laughter and music faded as they faded, like the memory of a weird dream, off into the chilly night.

Now the living and the dead stood facing each other, everyone staring and staring and no one saying a word. But what could the living and the dead say to each other? Where would they begin?

"You're just loving this, aren't you?" I said to my sister.

"You wanted excitement," she answered, her eyes twinkling.

Eventually, the dead began to wander away. They left the gym and the houses too. They went back to the cemetery and re-interred themselves. And the town grew quiet.

Then the people went home in silence. They crawled into their beds and pulled up the covers. But I doubt that anyone slept much on the evening of that Harvest Fest.

Now I can't say things in Millsap Hollow changed too much after the Parade of Night. Most people still weren't interested in hanging out in the cemetery. And we didn't sit around and talk about how our great-great-great grandparents won the Spanish American War.

But that was the last year anyone wished anyone a happy Harvest Fest. They never again tried to cancel Halloween. We had our candy and our costume parties. And the only beasts that roamed the streets were little kids in rubber masks.

Some years, however, when the wind whips through the trees, you can just make out the distant pounding of the drums. You can feel it in your legs and in your stomach. It's rhythmic. Hypnotic. You fall into a kind of trance.

And you have to figure, up there on that hill in the middle of town, the dead are out of their graves, stomping and dancing and reveling in their night—their one night—their All Hallow's Eve.

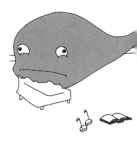

ELEVEN

Down, Down, Down

Peter McBower hated small places. His house was too small. His school was too small. He even felt that the very mountains that surrounded his hometown were closing in on him.

Peter's father was a coal miner, and so was his brother. In fact, the McBower men had toiled in the coal mines of eastern Kentucky for a hundred years. Peter's grandfather died of the black lung disease before Peter was even born. Now his father lay in bed, hacking and coughing as his frail body sank ever deeper into the mattress.

The company doctor said it was the coal dust, and there was nothing anyone could do once a man had swallowed his fill.

But a brighter future awaited Peter. He was a good student. He read all the books the

181

family could afford, from the flaking leather-bound Bible to the tattered editions of Mr. Shakespeare, Mr. Hawthorne, and Mr. Twain.

His mother wanted him to finish high school and go to college. He'd be the first McBower with an education. But more importantly he'd escape the mine—that horrible place, dark and damp, and so deep in the ground. It was so cramped and so small, with black walls, a black ceiling, and a black floor. Peter could cause himself to hyperventilate just by thinking about it.

"You just keep studying, boy," the old man said when he first got sick. "We'll make do."

The quitting whistle blew every evening at twilight, and sent Peter's brother tramping home to supper. Sean McBower would stamp into the tiny house, bringing with him the dank smell of the deep, deep earth. After the meal Peter would stay at the table and read, while Sean sat across the room, his fierce blue eyes staring out of a face blackened by the coal.

"Wash up, son," his mother would say.

And Sean would rub his face with a damp cloth, and go out on the porch to smoke a cigarette. All the coal miners smoked cigarettes, which only made them cough even harder.

Peter's brother was fifteen when he went down into the mines. The coal company raised the rent on their house every year, and the prices at the company store were always going up. His father's wages just hadn't been enough anymore.

At first Sean smiled and shrugged, saying he always knew he'd end up in the mines, so he might just as well make an early start of it. But after a month or so he began to change. His father had spent nearly half his life under the ground and it looked like mining was going to be the death of him. But the harsh work never seemed to affect the old man the way it did his eldest son.

Sean hardly laughed or smiled anymore, and he never had the time or energy to do anything fun. He and Peter used to go fishing together, and sometimes they'd go down to the tracks and chuck rocks at the trains. Now the little free time Sean had was spent in the company of a rough group of young miners. And whenever they caught Peter unawares they always gave him a good drubbing. His big brother just didn't stick up for him anymore.

Peter was in school when the whistle blew. Only it was mid-morning, much too early for the lunch whistle. Everyone knew what that meant.

"Remain calm," the teacher urged, as her students clambered out of the small schoolhouse.

They milled down toward the sound of the shrieking whistle, down toward the coal mine and the gathering crowd. Their mothers were there. The foremen and engineers were there. They all looked worried.

Soon word came around that it was a cave-in, and several young miners were trapped. Everyone knew Jim Rooney and Bill Franks were buried. And there were whispers that Fritz Schweitzer and Hank Carpenter had also been in the section that collapsed. Then someone started a rumor that young Sean McBower had been seen working alongside Schweitzer.

A train of men armed with picks and shovels began receding into the mouth of the mine.

In an hour's time they knew for certain. Some miners went and fetched Peter's father from his sickbed. They carried him out in a rocking chair, and the foreman came up and whispered in his ear. The old man withered.

"He said it's gonna be hours," he told Peter and his mother. "Maybe days. The whole southeast shaft is collapsed."

Peter's mother shuddered and sobbed.

"You best take her home, boy," his father said.

And standing there under the brilliant sunlight, Peter knew no matter how many times that old sun set and rose his brother wouldn't come home—not ever again.

After the funeral, Peter and his parents sat in the kitchen in silence. It'd been more than a week since the cave-in. It took them that long to recover the bodies. Then they stuck the boys in pine boxes and buried them again, on the same mountain and in the same dirt.

Peter's father sipped his coffee and coughed into his fist. It wouldn't be long before he'd have to crawl back under his blankets. Peter's mother simply sat, staring into space.

"The company man said we'll get compensated for our loss," the old man said at last. "But it won't be much. Not enough to live on. Not enough to . . ."

He didn't say anything more, but Peter knew what he meant. His parents never said it in so many words, but it was the only way. They had to make ends meet. Another McBower was destined for the mines.

Peter went and saw the foreman the next day.

"I'm sorry about your brother, son," said the big yellow-haired man. "He was a good boy."

Then he offered Peter the job. He'd start the next morning, well before sunup, when the whistle blew.

Peter spent the rest of the afternoon out by the tracks. He sat high up on a ridge and tossed pebbles down onto the tops of the freight cars as they shuffled past. He watched the downward progress of the sun, as it slid

out of the sky and melted orange in between the tops of the mountains.

When it was full dark he got up and started to run. He ran down through the hills and across the valley. He breathed deep and tried to fill his lungs with all the air in the world. His heart pounded in his chest and his feet flew free over the carpet of green. He felt he could go on like this forever and never turn back.

But that was a boyish fantasy.

Soon his legs got tired. Soon he was winded and doubled over, with all the air he'd ever sucked in expiring from his lungs in hot, doglike panting breaths.

He stumbled home like a drunkard.

His mother was sitting by the stove, staring through the small kitchen window. Peter didn't want to talk to her and tell her everything would be all right, even though he knew he should. He went straight to his cot instead, and lay for several hours without ever really sleeping.

The next morning the old woman was still sitting by the stove. Her back was turned toward Peter, and he saw that her shoulders were trembling. The old man's lunch pail was packed and waiting for Peter on the table. He picked it up and made his way out into the moonless dark.

The air was crisp and cold as was often the case in the mountain mornings. Men were making their way toward the mine in smoking, chattering groups of twos and threes.

Peter trudged alone.

At the mine, the foreman greeted him by handing him a pickax. A few minutes later, the whistle blew.

There was a long train of rail cars sitting on a track that disappeared into the mouth of the mine. Some of the cars held bins in which the coal would be loaded, others offered flat spaces on which the men could lie on their stomachs and ride down into the blackness.

"You get on there in the front, son," said the foreman, steering Peter to the head of the train. "New men have to work in the deepest part of the mine."

Reluctantly, Peter did as he was told. The flat rail car was cold and hard. He lay on it, clutching his pickax and staring into the gaping black maw of the mine. Once all the men were aboard, the little train chugged to life, the engine snorting smoke and pushing the other cars forward. The little wheels went click, click, clack on the tracks, like the wheels of a roller coaster, and Peter slid face first down into the darkness.

He couldn't believe how steep the descent was, and at times it seemed as though he was traveling straight down. The man behind him had a lantern, but the light it cast only illuminated the tunnel's ceiling. And the deeper the

train went, the lower that ceiling seemed to sink, until Peter couldn't lift his head for fear that it'd bump against the supporting timbers and cause a cave-in.

It was becoming hard to breathe. The air was thin and rife with sooty coal dust that hadn't settled after yesterday's labor. Peter began to cough.

At last the train ground to a halt in a small chamber, and several of the miners climbed off the cars and set to work with their shovels and pickaxes. Peter started to follow suit, but the man behind him grabbed his ankle.

"Not so fast, kid," he said in a familiar voice. "This ain't our stop."

Soon the train was moving again. Click, click, clack, and down deeper Peter went, puzzling over just whom it was behind him and trying to get a breath of breathable air. The rails shifted with a rusty screech of iron and the train turned onto a new track, and dropped ever deeper into the belly of the mountain.

Peter tried to breathe through his shirt, but it was no good. He could feel the flinty dust coating his lungs. He coughed harder.

The tunnel walls and ceiling seemed to be closing in. And if the little train went much deeper, Peter was convinced it'd get wedged between the layers of dirt and rock. But on it went. Click, click, clack.

"Will we be able to hear the lunch whistle this far down?" Peter asked, looking over his shoulder and trying to catch a glimpse of the other miner's face.

"No," said the man, who was shrouded in shadows.

Peter wanted to ask how they'd know when it was time to go to lunch if they weren't going to hear the whistle. But something—perhaps the iciness with which the man had answered his first question—made the words stick in his throat.

Then with a squealing of brakes the train lurched to a final stop. It was the end of the line.

The ceiling was so low Peter had to stoop over to work. He swung his pickax at the waist, as the man next to him—whose face he couldn't see for the dim light and the floppy brim of the fellow's tattered hat—shoveled the coal out. A third man, further down the line, received the ore in a bucket and passed it along to the last man, who deposited it into the waiting bin. All of the men worked in silence in the shadows, of which there were plenty in the sooty little cave. Peter didn't try to make conversation, either, as he assumed it was the way of miners to toil and never talk.

Besides, he was too busy to talk. The man next to him scooped up the coal as quickly as he could knock it loose. Before long the pickax

189

started to feel like an anchor, weighing upon his arms and sending shockwaves down his spine with every swing and strike.

And then there was the dust. The horrible black, sooty stink that exploded up into his face and matted his hair with every swing and strike. Swing and strike. Swing and strike.

As they dredged the ore from between the crevices of rock and dirt, they gradually moved deeper into the pit and further from the train. Swing, strike, and step to the left. Swing, strike, and step to the left. And it wasn't long before Peter could no longer see train nor tracks nor, for the maze of tunnels and hollows, tell which way the railroad lay.

Of course he didn't realize how far from the tracks he'd ventured until the pain in his back, the crick in his neck, and the soreness in his arms got the better of him. He set the pickax down and peeled his fingers from the handle.

"It has *got* to be lunchtime," he said to the strange man with the shovel.

Then, glancing about, he suddenly realized how far they'd strayed from the train.

"Hey, how do we get back to the tracks from here?" he asked.

The miner only stared at him from under the brim of the floppy hat. Peter could just make out the green glint of the man's eyes. The rest of his face was a pool of darkness, and his clothes were tattered and filthy, even by the standards of a coalminer.

But, still, Peter couldn't shake the feeling of familiarity.

"Do I know you from somewhere, mister?" he asked. "Are you a friend of my father's, maybe?"

The man only lifted his arm, indicating that Peter should follow him down a tunnel. "This way," he said in his emotionless tone.

The other miners Peter had been working with were already moving down the tunnel. And he certainly didn't want to get left all alone, so he quickly started after them. But pretty soon the ceiling became quite low and he had to crawl. The timbers and dirt gave way to solid rock as the tunnel led into a natural cave.

Peter was having trouble breathing too. "Are you sure this is the way?" he called to the man in front of him. It seemed they should've come upon the tracks before now.

"Just a little farther," said the man, the soles of his boots disappearing into the darkness as he shambled deeper into the tunnel.

Peter kept following, but he couldn't shake the feeling that they were moving in the wrong direction. And the tunnel's ceiling sank lower still, so that he had to crawl with his

head hung low. Soon he found he couldn't catch his breath at all and had to stop.

He rolled over on his back and pushed on the rock face above his head, like a man who'd been buried alive pushing on the lid of his coffin. The lantern light faded with the others as they continued down the tunnel. Peter didn't want to be left alone in the dark, desperately clawing at a ceiling that would never give an inch.

"Wait!" he shouted. "Don't leave me here!"

"Hurry," the cold voice echoed back. "Just a little farther."

Somehow Peter gathered the strength to roll back over and drag himself a little farther. But he knew it was wrong. They were moving downward and not back up.

He saw the light ahead, and kept moving until he caught up. The others finally seemed to be waiting for him. They were crouched in a semi-circle in a small chamber at the end of the tunnel, which seemed to Peter to be a dead end.

He crawled out of the tunnel and joined them in the chamber. But the lantern light was shining in his eyes, and he still couldn't see their faces. They were all staring at him, though. He could feel it. They gave him the creeps. And now that he was closer to them they all seemed familiar.

"Where do we go now?" he asked.

The man in the floppy hat only pointed to a crevice in the wall of the chamber—a crevice no more than a foot wide.

"You've got to be joking," Peter said.

But the man shook his head and said, "Just a little farther."

One by one the miners slipped into the crevice, oozing between the layers of rock with the greatest of ease.

Peter knew he shouldn't try to follow. He knew it wasn't the way out. A four-year-old kid would've known it wasn't the way out. But something compelled him to keep going deeper. Something he didn't quite understand, although he knew he'd had a similar feeling the night before when he went home instead of running away.

He pulled himself head first into the crevice. It was dark and the air was very thin. He scratched with his fingernails and moved by inches, scraping his back against the rock above. His heart pounded, the sweat poured off him. He thought of the rock and dirt that lay below him, stretching all the way to the earth's molten core. And he thought of all that lay above him: a mountain of rock and dirt and filthy black coal. The one expanse seemed as great as the other, and he was like an ant caught in a tiny crack in the middle of it all.

He felt certain he was about to get stuck. He had to suck his chest and stomach in to get through where the crevice was particularly tight. And just when he thought he'd reached a point where the crevice simply wasn't wide enough, several clammy hands reached in and pulled him the rest of the way out.

Now they all stood very close to him in a little hollowed out place no bigger than a deep sea-diving bell. The man in the floppy hat turned the lantern up, and the yellow light illuminated their faces.

They were ghastly and pale, with their flesh rotting away in big discolored chunks. Worms wove strange patterns, wriggling out of a nostril here and into an eye-socket there. But the maggots were worst of all: they moved in teeming white masses up the necks and over the faces, devouring skin and muscle as they went. Some of the filthy little insects disappeared into the men's hair, while great scores of them went pouring into the gaping mouths.

The men, however, didn't even seem to notice.

Peter recognized them all: Rooney, Franks, Schweitzer, and Carpenter. They were his brother's old gang, and the young men who'd been buried with Sean the week before.

Then Peter saw his brother. He was sitting in the corner, his fierce blue eyes staring out of a face every bit as cadaverous as the others.

Slowly, the lantern was extinguished, and the dead miners began to close in on Peter. He opened his mouth to cry out, but no sound came. Not that it mattered. He knew no amount of screaming would help him anyway.

His big brother just didn't stick up for him anymore.

TWELVE

Orphan Asylum

Helen didn't remember much about the car crash, although when she shut her eyes she still saw the blinding headlights of the big rig truck. Her family's sedan was run off the road and down the embankment it went; Helen's whole world tumbling and turning to black.

When she woke up, she found herself in a place called St. Dymphna's Orphan Asylum. Her brother and sister were there as well—Jacob in the boy's dormitory and Cecily ten beds down.

"It's best to keep siblings separate," said Miss Mercy, the headmistress of St. Dymphna's. "It makes things easier in the long run."

"But Cecily's scared of the dark," Helen protested. "Can't she have the bed next to mine?"

But Miss Mercy wouldn't even consider it. She said she didn't want Helen and Cecily whispering together all night long.

Miss Mercy was a tall angular woman with an impossibly long face. She wore an old-fashioned dress with a high collar that covered her neck. Her skin was completely colorless, and her hair matched it perfectly. She floated up and down the hallways and in and out of the dormitories, a lantern in her hand. She never seemed to sleep.

"Your parents are no longer with you," Miss Mercy told Helen. "You're all on your own now. And the sooner you accept that the better off you'll be."

As peculiar and harsh as Miss Mercy was, however, she seemed a perfect match for St. Dymphna's. The orphanage was a great crumbling block of a building stuck smack dab in the middle of the city. There was no electricity and not a drop of hot water. The other kids were sullen and sickly and, try as she might, Helen could barely get any one of them to say more than two words. They shuffled about, responding like robots when Miss Mercy rang the big bell in the courtyard.

This all seemed quite strange to Helen. But nothing was as strange as the city that existed just outside the walls of St. Dymphna's. When Helen gazed down from the window of the girl's dormitory, the bustling street, with its ebb and flow of people and cars, seemed faded and far away. She felt as though she was watching a really old movie—one where everything's all washed out and the people move too quickly.

The walls around her were solid. Miss Mercy and the other kids, as pale as they were, seemed quite real. Yet the city that surrounded them was as foggy as a half-forgotten dream.

"Helen, what are you looking at?" Cecily whispered from the darkness of the dormitory.

"Nothing," Helen snapped, pulling back the curtain. Her sister had startled her. "What are you doing out of bed?"

"I'm worried about Jacob," she said. "We hardly ever get to see him."

"I know," Helen said. "I'm worried too."

The girls only got to speak to their brother in the dining hall. Even then they could only whisper together for a few minutes before Miss Mercy saw them and clapped her hands for silence. But in the short time they had, Jacob did manage to tell his sisters some very upsetting news.

"I'm gonna be adopted," he said one evening at supper.

"Oh, that's good," said Cecily. "I can't wait to get out of here and go live in a house with a nice family."

"No, you don't get it," Jacob moaned. *"We're* not being adopted. *I'm* being adopted. They only want me. And they're horrible. I can't even begin to describe them." He seemed very frightened.

Helen could hardly believe it. She never dreamed she could lose her brother on top of losing both parents. "They can't split us up," she cried. "It has to be illegal or something."

"There's no law in this place," Jacob said. He was becoming frantic. "You guys still don't know where we are, do you? There's stuff I need to tell you."

"About what?" the girls pressed.

"About this place. About that weird couple that wants to adopt me. And even . . . about us."

Naturally that was the exact moment Miss Mercy chose to ring the bell and send everyone scuffling back to the dormitories. Helen and her siblings knew they couldn't linger.

"We'll talk more tomorrow," Helen told her brother as they drifted apart in the crowd. "Just don't panic."

Helen didn't want her brother and sister to worry, so she did her best to hide her emotions. She managed to stay pretty calm on the outside, but inside she was feeling both afraid and angry. *If that old bat thinks she's going to separate us,* she thought. But she didn't finish the thought, because she had no idea how she could stop Miss Mercy from pulling them all apart. Still, she had to try.

"You go on back to the dorm," she said to Cecily. "I'll be there in a little bit."

She caught up with Miss Mercy outside her office.

"What is it, child?" the old woman asked.

"Is it true?" Helen demanded. "Are you really going to separate my brother and sister and me?"

Miss Mercy looked almost regretful for a moment, but then her face hardened. "It's for the best," she said. "You can't hold on to your past lives anymore than you can return to them."

"What is that supposed to mean?" Helen shouted. "Me, Cecily, and Jake need one another more now than ever. It's our parents who've died, not us."

Miss Mercy lurched forward and grabbed Helen by the shoulders. Her face was like a fish, skinny as a hatchet, with big googlie eyeballs stuck on either side. "You foolish girl," she hissed. "Don't you realize where you are?"

"Let me go," Helen cried, struggling ferociously.

"Get back to your dormitory," the old woman said, dragging her down the hall. "I have work to do."

Helen finally managed to wrench free. Then she ran past several girls and collapsed face forward on her cot. Cecily tapped her on the back.

"Helen, Helen," she whispered. "I'm scared."

Helen didn't look up. She didn't want her little sister to see her. She didn't want anyone to see her. For the first time since the accident that robbed her of her parents, Helen Ann Lucas was crying.

She didn't sleep at all that night. She ended up sitting at the window, staring at the scene below and puzzling over the strange things Jacob and Miss Mercy had said. The room behind her was pitch dark and filled with sleeping girls. But the window in front of her glowed as silver as a movie screen.

Five stories below the cars nosed along, stopping and starting like marching soldiers. She watched a fat delivery truck break ranks and swerve into an alley. The people were on the sidewalks beneath the sparkle of the street lamps. They seemed fuzzy and unreal and moved not unlike the cars. The whole scene blurred together and made Helen feel dizzy.

Then she saw a young man on horseback. He was cantering up the street as if the congested city were nothing more than a cow town. She watched him for a minute, but soon something else caught her eye.

The crowd below her window had gathered around a man and a woman who appeared to be playing tug of war. Helen squinted hard and saw what it was they were both pulling on. It was the woman's handbag. The man was a purse snatcher and the game of tug of war was no game at all.

The man wrenched the purse free and went running in the opposite direction. The crowd simply parted and let him pass. The woman appeared to be crying, but no one tried to help her.

Then there was a whistle—a loud shriek that reached even Helen's ears. The horse was coming on at a gallop now, the dashing young man bouncing in the saddle. And Helen could see that he was wearing a blue coat with brass buttons and a blue hat. Suddenly the young man and his horse didn't seem so out of place. He was a mounted policeman, and he was gaining rapidly on the purse snatcher.

The thief ducked into the alley where the delivery truck was parked. The driver had already made his drop and was eager to continue his rounds. He revved the engine and floored the gas pedal. The purse snatcher managed to dive out of the way of the speeding vehicle, but the mounted policeman wasn't so lucky.

The horse had just rounded the corner when the truck came rumbling out of the alley. The poor animal reared and neighed,

nearly throwing its rider. Helen covered her eyes. Then there was a horrible squealing of brakes, followed by a prominent thud. It was the most awful sound Helen had heard since the night of her family's car accident.

She didn't want to look, but not to look was even worse. The poor man. The poor horse. She peeked between her fingers.

It was as she feared. The policeman was on the ground. He'd been thrown, but he wasn't seriously hurt. Unfortunately, the same couldn't be said for his partner. The horse lay in a heap, completely motionless. The young policeman leaned over the animal. He seemed to be crying.

Helen wanted to look away. Like most girls, she'd always liked horses, and she hated to see one die in such a terrible accident. She was about to close the curtain, but then something very peculiar happened.

The horse stood up. At least that's what Helen thought she saw. It rose up on all fours, a beautiful palomino with diamond shaped spots. It glowed bright and pranced about as radiant as any painting Helen had ever seen.

But no one below seemed to notice the horse's sudden recovery. The policeman was still crying, and everyone was still staring down at the broken body in the street. Yes, it was still there, as if it weren't really the horse's dead body at all, but some kind of cocoon that the real horse had just stepped out of.

The palomino raced up and down in a flurry of excitement.

"Oh, Bayard," the policeman cried, still leaning over the broken body.

Helen felt sorry for him. She wanted to throw open the window and shout, "There is your pretty horse! It's alive and free. It's not that empty shell lying on the ground."

But before she could say anything the horse ran headlong toward the gates of St. Dymphna's. It disappeared from view as it came closer to the building, then Helen heard the clattering of hooves in the courtyard. She rushed out into the hall and leaned over the railing.

The palomino was trotting circles in the courtyard, snorting and neighing in its confusion over the sudden turn of events. The animal appeared quite solid and real now, completely unlike the faded people out on the street. Helen started toward the stairs, eager to get a closer look at the pretty horse, but Miss Mercy beat her to the quick.

Only Miss Mercy wasn't interested in admiring the palomino. She sprang from her office brandishing a broom. "Shoo, shoo," she shouted, waving the broom and flailing about like a scarecrow in a storm. "You don't belong here, you beast! Out! Out, I say!"

The horse shied from the broom and galloped to the opposite end of the courtyard.

"Leave him alone," Helen yelled. "He's just been hit by a truck."

"You keep quiet, Helen Ann Lucas," the headmistress said. "This orphanage is no home to beasts of burden."

By now the other kids were staggering sleepily from the dormitories to see what all the fuss was about. They rubbed their eyes and gazed down at the scene in the courtyard in disbelief. Miss Mercy had cornered the palomino and was now unceremoniously slapping its hindquarters with the broom and shouting, "Out, you beast! Out!"

"Stop that!" Helen demanded, fighting her way through the crowd around the stairs.

"I told you to keep quiet," Miss Mercy shrieked. "This animal has to go."

"But that's no way to treat him. Why don't you try being kind. His name is Bayard, not 'you beast'."

But Miss Mercy was hearing none of it, and as she continued to deal roughly with the policeman's horse, the big bell began to ring all of its own accord. The kids in the hall started making their way back to the dormitories. The headmistress had them perfectly conditioned to the bell.

Helen was pushed and jostled by the crowd. She tried to wrestle her way closer to the railing, so she could get another look at what was going on in the courtyard, but some kid bumped into her from behind. "Watch it, you clumsy little . . . " she said, whirling about and coming face to face with her brother.

Tears were welling in Jacob's eyes. "You gotta help me, Helen," he said. Then he just managed to push a crumpled piece of paper into her hand before he was swept off among a crowd of other boys.

Back in the girl's dorm Helen unfolded the paper and had her worst fears confirmed.

Helen,

They're coming to get me the day after tomorrow, just before sunup. I'm so afraid of them I don't know what to do. And worst of all, Miss Mercy says I'll never see you or Cecily ever again.

Goodbye forever,

—Jacob

All the next day Helen tried to devise a way to keep her brother from being adopted. He seemed so afraid of the people who were coming to claim him. *Who are they?* she wondered. *How can they be so cruel as to want to separate us?* She considered going to see Miss Mercy again, but knew it was hopeless. The headmistress was the cruelest one of all. She was mean to everyone and everything, even frightened horses.

At suppertime Helen finally made up her mind. She and her brother and sister would simply have to run away. "We're coming to get you right after lights out," she whispered to Jacob, while pretending to pass the asparagus. "Then we're all getting out of here."

Jacob looked pretty shaken up, but he managed to nod his head.

Miss Mercy began her patrol at the same hour every evening. She locked all the doors in the courtyard, then came upstairs and conducted the head counts—first the boys, then the girls. Helen had her clocked down to the second.

She didn't move a muscle when she felt the evil eye watching her. She pretended to be asleep, and waited for the headmistress to finish the count. Then, as the door creaked shut, she slowly opened her eyes. The room was very dark.

Helen eased out from under the blankets and measured her steps until she came to her sister's cot. "Cecily," she whispered, nudging the sleeping form. "Come on. We have to hurry."

The girls crept down the hall and into the boy's dormitory. Jacob wasn't hard to find. He was sitting Indian-style on his cot, with his face buried in his hands.

"Jake," Helen called, as quietly as possible. "Are you ready? Let's go."

Jacob uncovered his face. He seemed very sad and hopeless. "There's something I have to tell you guys," he said.

"There's no time," Helen insisted. "Tell us later. We've gotta out of here now!"

Footsteps rang out in the hall.

"She's coming," Cecily whimpered. "She must have heard you!"

Helen rushed over to the window and threw open the sash. "Quick," she told her brother and sister. "Out onto the ledge."

"Are you crazy?" Cecily asked. "We'll break our necks." She stared past the fluttering curtains to the narrow precipice of the ledge. The sidewalk was a blur of concrete some fifty feet below.

"We don't have any choice," Helen insisted. "We'll work our way along the ledge, then shimmy down the rain spout." She grabbed ahold of her sister's britches. "Go!" she demanded. "I've got you."

Reluctantly, Cecily crawled out onto the ledge. Helen turned and reached her free hand out to her brother. She was flabbergasted to find him still sitting on his cot. "Jake, what are you thinking?" she cried. "We've got to get out of here!"

"But, Helen," he whined. "There's something I have to tell you."

The footsteps grew louder. Someone was just outside the door.

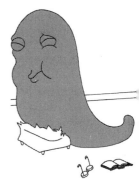

"Save it!" Helen hissed. "Do you want to get stuck living with those people, or are you coming with us?"

Just as the door began to creak inward, Jacob ambled across the room and took his sister's hand. They stepped out onto the ledge and plastered themselves against the brickwork on either side of the window. Cecily clutched her sister's hand and shivered like a wet puppy. "Try to be still," Helen whispered.

They tried to make like gargoyles, clinging to the ledge and holding their breath.

The footsteps approached the window and Miss Mercy's narrow face nosed out into the night. She held her lantern in front of her, looked to the street below, then to the stars above. Helen thought she detected the slightest trace of a smile on the headmistress's face, but before she could be certain the old woman withdrew and slammed the window shut.

The vibration nearly sent them all tumbling off the ledge. They held on to one another, however, and just managed to keep their balance.

Once they regained level footing they began creeping toward the corner of the building. The rain spout proved to be rather rickety and rusty, but it was the only avenue of escape.

"There's no way I can climb down that thing," Cecily complained. "I'll fall for sure."

"We don't have any choice," Helen said. "I'll go first. Just follow me and do what I do."

Helen reached around her sister and grabbed the spout. Then she swung from the ledge and clung to the precarious metal chute, wrapping her hands, knees, and even her feet around it as best she could. "See, it's not so hard," she said, although she was actually feeling quite dizzy.

Gradually she began to slide downward, loosening her grip ever so slightly and inching toward the street. "This isn't so hard," she repeated, doing her best impersonation of the Little Engine That Could.

She looked up at her brother and sister, who were still standing on the ledge, and called for them to follow her. That's when something unexpected happened.

Helen lost her grip on the spout and fell. At least, if she'd had time to think about it during her rapid descent, it would have occurred to her that she must have lost her grip. After all that was the only reasonable explanation. Never mind the fact that Helen could have sworn her hands had suddenly passed through the spout as if it'd been made of smoke instead of metal.

She free fell fifty feet and landed on the hard ground just inside the gates of St. Dymphna's. "I must be dead," she said to herself, "because I don't feel any pain."

"That's what I've been trying to tell you," said her brother. He stood above her, as if he'd simply floated down from the fifth story ledge.

"How did you get down here so fast?" Helen asked.

"The same way you did," Jacob replied. "Only I let myself fall on purpose."

"What are you talking about? Are you saying we're *both* dead?"

Jacob sighed. "It's what I've been trying to tell you all along, Sis. We're all dead. You, me, and Cecily. Only we didn't get killed falling off a ledge."

Cecily was still perched fifty feet above them and staring down with eyes wide in disbelief.

Terrible revelation suddenly dawned on Helen. "The car crash," she whispered. "Mom and Dad weren't killed. It was the three of us who got killed."

Jacob nodded his head. "This orphanage is a home for kids who've died before their parents. We're ghosts, Helen. And the people who want to adopt me are ghosts too. Only they're not like us. They know they're ghosts, and they like it."

"What do you mean?" Helen asked.

But her brother didn't get a chance to answer. Miss Mercy was coming down the path. Her face looked as though it'd been chiseled from stone. "Now you know the truth," she said looking down on Helen. "And now you may say goodbye to your brother."

There was a great roar and a big black car pulled up on the street outside the main gate. It was an old fashioned car, round and humped and ugly, like a giant beetle. There were a bunch of tin cans tied to the bumper and the words *Just Married* were written in soap on the back window. The other windows were as black as the chrome finish, and neither Helen nor Jacob could see inside. But the really peculiar thing about the large automobile was the way it seemed to be changing shape before their very eyes. One minute it looked new and shiny, as though it had just rolled off the showroom floor. The next minute it looked like a heap of wreckage, all scarred, twisted, and bent.

Helen and Jacob rubbed their eyes, trying to make out which car was the real car. But before they could figure it out the doors swung open to reveal a darkness as smothering as the inside of a coffin.

"It's them," Jacob whispered. "I'm doomed."

Helen scrambled to her feet, but there was nowhere to run. Miss Mercy stood behind them, and the car loomed in front. Besides, Cecily was still stuck up on the ledge, more frightened and confused than ever.

A man in a black suit stepped out of the car on the driver's side. He was tall and gaunt, and wore a vacant smile, like the smile of a dummy in a wax museum. He had buckteeth, hollow cheek bones, and skin so bone-white it looked like his skeleton was about to burst through. He walked around to the passenger's side of the car and offered his hand to someone inside.

A long thin arm, covered in a white glove, reached from the darkness and accepted the man's hand. Then the woman stepped out into the light of the street lamps, and Helen nearly fainted.

She wore a flowing wedding gown, radiant and white, with her face completely shrouded in a veil—the darkness behind it was overwhelming. Only her steely gray eyes shone forth, piercing and hypnotic. And you would swear there was no face around those eyes. There could be nothing in that darkness—no flesh, no blood, nothing remotely human— save those haunting eyes. She was terrible and beautiful at the same time. Just one glimpse of her made you remember every time you were ever alone and afraid of the dark.

The man took her white-gloved arm in his and they floated over the sidewalk toward St. Dymphna's. The gate swung open with a squeal of rusty hinges and they drifted on in, gazing fixedly at poor Jacob.

Helen crossed in front of her brother, but she knew she wouldn't be able to protect him. Miss Mercy seized him by the shoulders and rooted him to the spot where he stood.

"Helen," she said, her sharp face peering down over the top of Jacob's head. "May I present Phineas and Phaedra Exeter. They're to be your brother's guardians from now 'til the end of eternity."

The man, still smiling, cocked his head like a parrot and said, "Well, hello, Helen." His voice was honeyed, like that of a phony preacher. "I'm sorry you're gonna lose your brother. But do understand that it's for the best."

"How can separating us be for the best?" Helen demanded.

"My beloved bride is heartbroken," explained Phineas Exeter. "For you see, we never got a chance to have a little boy of our own, seeing as how we perished on our wedding night."

The specter of a woman stared longingly at Jacob, her bridal gown swirling and shiny. Phaedra Exeter was little more than an empty dress.

Helen swallowed hard and summoned her courage. "Why not take all three of us?" she asked. "You could have a boy and two girls." As horrible as the Exeters were, she couldn't let Jacob face an eternity with them on his own.

"We only want the boy," rasped an otherworldly voice from somewhere deep in the emptiness behind Phaedra Exeter's veil.

"But why?" shouted Helen, near the point of tears. "Why only Jake?"

"Because," grinned Phineas Exeter, "it will make him very sad to lose his sisters. And we'd like very much for him to be sad."

Helen wanted to scream. But she could only watch in horror as Miss Mercy shoved Jacob into the cold clutches of the Exeters.

They took him by the arms, and when they touched him he seemed to change. He grew paler and withered, and for the first time he appeared to Helen as he actually was: the unhappy ghost of a little boy.

By now Cecily had made her way back off the ledge. She raced downstairs and burst through the front doors, shouting at the Exeters to set her brother free. But there was nothing she or Helen could do.

The ghastly couple drifted backward, pulling Jacob with them. The gate swung shut behind them as they passed back over the sidewalk and into the funeral blackness of their car. Then the engine erupted with a ferocious roar and they sped off down the street, passing straight through another car and causing it to swerve into a lamp post.

Helen and Cecily were left standing on the weedy patch of ground in front of St. Dymphna's. They both wished they had done more to save their brother, but what could they have done? They knew they were ghosts now, yet they still felt like a couple of helpless kids. Something—perhaps some power of Miss Mercy's—prevented them from passing through the gate. But even if they could escape Miss Mercy and the grounds of St. Dymphna's, they couldn't fly through the air behind the Exeters speeding car like a pair of cartoon ghosts—at least not so far as they knew.

Miss Mercy stood before them, the blackness of her eyes as cold and empty as the blackness behind Phaedra Exeter's veil. "Get back to your dormitories," she spat.

Helen and Cecily had no choice but to obey.

"Is that what's gonna happen to us too?" Cecily wondered, as they climbed the stairs. "We're just gonna wait here 'til a couple of ghouls come to take us to live in some haunted house somewhere?"

Helen didn't answer her sister. She was thinking about her mother and father. They were alive somewhere—back home, she guessed—and could no more help their children than any of the people on the outside. Those people who seemed so faded and distant only because they were alive, while everyone inside St. Dymphna's was dead. Helen

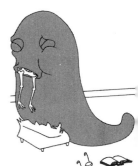

thought about the young policeman and wondered if he might be willing to help them, if only he could.

That's when it dawned on her. Maybe there was a way she and Cecily could catch the Exeter's car. "No, we're not going to wait around here," she told her sister. "Not for another minute. Come on!"

"Where are we going?" Cecily asked, as Helen dragged her along by her wrist. "How are we going to get past Miss Mercy and over the gate?"

"Maybe there's a way," Helen said, as they stumbled down the stairs and ran outside. She scoured the grounds, searching this way and that, and pulling her sister in her wake.

"What are you looking for?" Cecily cried.

"You'll know it when we see it," said Helen.

She looked for hoof prints and signs of foraging, but soon realized the ghost of a horse wouldn't leave hoof prints or need to forage for food. Finally she spotted him in the side yard. He was cowering in a stand of leafy trees, hiding from Miss Mercy's broom. "Bayard," Helen said softly, approaching him on tip toe. "I thought you might still be here somewhere."

The palomino's spirit, frightened and confused after being hit by the truck, had nowhere else to go. So he'd remained behind the gates of St. Dymphna's and away from the lights and noise of the city.

Helen touched his snout. "It's okay, boy. We're your friends."

The horse softly snorted his approval and allowed himself to be patted.

"He's beautiful," said Cecily, admiring his diamond shaped spots.

"I TOLD YOU TO GO BACK TO YOUR DORMITORY!" Miss Mercy's voice split the air like thunder, freezing Helen and Cecily where they stood.

Bayard whinnied and reared, flailing his hooves like crazy.

"No!" Helen told him. "Calm down! You have to help us."

Miss Mercy came storming toward them, her hatchet face cutting through the darkness like the prow of a battleship. "You will pay dearly for your disobedience," she warned the girls.

Bayard was still bucking and whinnying. Helen tried desperately to soothe him, but her words simply weren't enough. Then something peculiar happened. The horse looked right at Miss Mercy and back at the girls. That's when he stopped bucking, lowered his head and allowed the two sisters to climb on his back.

"Get off that animal at once!" Miss Mercy railed.

But Helen clung fast to Bayard's mane, with Cecily clinging to her waist. "You said this orphanage is 'no home to beasts of burden'," she reminded the headmistress. "So we're getting him out of here, just like you wanted."

They galloped over the weedy ground, bound for the gate. Miss Mercy shrieked and tried to snatch them from the palomino's back. But she had no hold on the horse and it sped past her. Helen and Cecily couldn't go beyond the gate, but no such spell bound Bayard. He leapt into the air and passed through the bars, carrying the girls along on his back.

Then they were on the street, with Miss Mercy's screams trailing far behind. They raced around the cars, the palomino's hooves clattering on the pavement with gathering speed. The horse seemed to understand that he wasn't limited any longer. He jumped a Volkswagen and even passed straight through the middle of a bus. They entered through the big, greasy engine, then waded on up the aisle between the seats of sleeping passengers, and finally emerged from the windshield, leaving the driver to shudder and wonder at the sudden draft.

They galloped on and on, leaving the city and crossing into the countryside. They thundered down winding lanes, across bridges, and over hills. Helen urged Bayard to run ever faster, until the road was a blur and the stars seemed to streak across the sky.

At last they saw the car. It was several yards ahead, disappearing and reappearing in the bends of the road. One minute it was the twisted wreck. The next minute it was shiny and new.

Bayard seemed to understand. He lowered his head and redoubled his speed. Cecily squeezed Helen as tight as she could.

They caught the Exeters' car at the top of a hill, and Bayard plunged in through the trunk. Helen felt as though she were inside a tomb. She couldn't see the horse's head as it poked up through the hood, but she and Cecily soon found themselves passing through the back seat. It was upholstered like a coffin, with fluffy white ruffles. Jacob was sitting among those ruffles, looking small and helpless, yet somehow relieved to see his sisters riding through the car on horseback.

Helen held Bayard's mane with one hand and reached out to her brother with the other. Jacob eagerly accepted his sister's hand and she began to pull him onto the palomino's back.

Phaedra Exeter, however, had other plans. She spun around in the passenger's seat, her gray eyes flashing from behind the veil. She grabbed Jacob's ankle in an icy cold grip and twisted it cruelly. Jacob cried out, more from sheer terror than from pain, and kicked feebly at the gloved hand.

Helen held onto her brother with all of her might, but Phaedra was incredibly strong. And Mr. Exeter did his part, speeding up and slowing down and making it almost impossible for Bayard to keep pace with the car.

"Jake!" Helen cried. But she could feel him slipping away.

She was desperate. And so she did something desperate. She let go of the horse's mane and snatched at the veil. She snatched at Phaedra Exeter's bridal veil and pulled it open like the curtain on a carnival freakshow.

For one split second the gray eyes were left floating in the terrible darkness. There was a great shriek of misery and the gloves shot up, covering the emptiness and leaving the eyes to flash between the white fingers.

Jacob slid onto Bayard's back behind his sisters and onward the horse charged. They moved through the front seat, into the dashboard and past the plunging pistons of the big engine.

Helen looked back at Mr. and Mrs. Exeter. For once Phineas wasn't smiling and his nightmare bride was sitting with her veil restored and her gray eyes filled with both wrath and longing. And Helen honestly couldn't say which emotion was more terrible to behold.

Bayard leapt off the road and galloped across a field, leaving the car farther and farther behind. Helen and her brother and sister had no idea where they were going. They were all on their own now, yet they knew they could always rely on one another. They trotted on, with the sun rising behind them and the leafy, flowering beauty of the earth opening before them in green and yellow and all the colors they saw when they were alive . . . and never really noticed.

THIRTEEN

In Shadows

The Madison family minivan rolled along over the rain soaked streets of the Garden District. The sky was inky black and shrouded in a blanket of clouds. The asphalt shimmered, every puddle, pothole, and swollen gutter reflecting the light from the street lamps and creating a weird kind of glow.

Laticia, the youngest of the three Madison daughters, was in big trouble. She had started a food fight in a fast food restaurant and left the place a mess. Now her mother had told her to go straight to her room as soon as the family got home. Never mind the fact that she hated her room and dreaded going to bed every night.

Mrs. Madison had stopped yelling, but Laticia could tell she was still fuming. She sat

rigid in the front passenger's seat, studying her daughter in the rear-view mirror.

Laticia clambered over the seat she was sharing with her sisters, her foot nearly brushing the side of Tamara's head, and flopped into the back of the van.

Tamara turned around and wagged her finger in her little sister's face. "You watch where you're swinging your big feet, Lottie," she warned. "We've put up with enough from you for one night."

Lottie was Laticia's nickname. Everyone in the family called her by it, but she didn't like it. Of course, there were a lot of things she didn't like about her family. She thought her parents were too strict—especially her mother. And both of her sisters—Tamara and Charise—treated her like a little kid. They thought they were so grown up, because they were in high school and had boyfriends, while Laticia hadn't even had her thirteenth birthday yet.

She lay on the floor of the van and gazed up through the rear window. The rain had stopped, and the moon was peeking through the clouds. Soon they'd pull up in the driveway of the moldy old house, and Laticia would have to go upstairs.

She dreaded spending yet another night in her new bedroom. She barely got any sleep in the creepy bed, with its big smothering canopy. She didn't like the closet, either. It was too dark and stank of old things. But the connecting bathroom was worst of all. It was so cold in there. And there was that mirror over the sink. It was a great big gaudy thing, with hundreds of little cracks around the edges.

Her mother called these kinds of things antiques, but Laticia hated them all. She wished they were still back at their old house, which was a newer house anyway. So what if it was smaller? At least she wouldn't be afraid to go to sleep at night.

Her daddy put the van in reverse and began backing up the long driveway. She could see her bedroom window high above. It looked gloomy and uninviting.

"Lottie," her mother called from the front seat. "I want you to march yourself right up to your room and into bed. And I don't want to hear so much as one word."

Laticia heard what her mother said, but found she couldn't respond. Her attention was riveted to her bedroom window, where something had just appeared. At first she saw only a dark shape, but that shape was definitely moving. Yet everyone who lived in the house, every member of the Madison family, was in the minivan.

Laticia screamed.

"Oh, what is it now?" her mother demanded.

Her sisters leaned over the seat to see what was the matter. But Laticia couldn't look away from the window. The thing in her room had just pressed its face against the glass and was peering out at her. It was horrible, like something that had escaped from a circus. The face seemed as big and round as the moon, and every last inch of it, except for the piercing eyes, was covered in coarse brown hair.

Laticia whimpered and gestured toward the window. But by the time the others looked, the face had vanished.

It took almost an hour for Laticia to calm down. She cried and fussed. She pled with her parents not to be sent to bed. She didn't want to set foot in that room ever again.

Her father searched the entire bedroom from top to bottom and found no intruder—hairy faced or clean-shaven.

"That settles it," Mrs. Madison said. "There is nothing in that bedroom for you to be afraid of, young lady."

Laticia still refused to budge. She stood in the middle of the living room, flat-out defying her mother, with her arms folded across her chest. Mrs. Madison could always inspire fear in her daughters. But the fear of mere punishment was nothing compared to the shear terror Laticia had felt at seeing that awful face.

"If you are not in that bedroom by the count of three," Mrs. Madison said, "I will carry you there myself. And you will remain in that bedroom until you forget what the inside of a mall even looks like."

Laticia knew her mother meant what she said. And as scared as she was, she couldn't bear the idea of having to spend even more time in her bedroom.

Mrs. Madison began to count, and on three Laticia bounded up the stairs. There was no one in her room, just as her father had promised. And for a moment or two, she hoped that it had all been a hallucination.

She knew she had to turn her bedroom light out, or her mother would come up and do it for her. But she could at least leave the bathroom light on, as she did every night. She liked to use it as a nightlight, although that wasn't the only reason she left it burning.

The bathroom, with its creepy mirror, faced her bed, and she couldn't stand to look into that mirror in the dark. She always swore there was something sinister there, reflected in the glass, its outline almost visible. She could probably see what it was if she ran into the bathroom and snapped the light back on. Only she didn't want to see what it was. So she kept the bathroom light on all night every night.

She turned the switch on the big lamp next to her bed and dove under the covers, pulling the gauzy canopy curtains closed around her. A rectangle of yellow light spilled out over

the floor in front of the bathroom, but the rest of the room was cast in shadows. And it was all of the things that might lurk in those shadows that kept Laticia from sleeping.

She was breathing heavily, her heart thumping in her chest. She lay on her back, her eyes wide open and staring at the shapes around her. Nothing seemed out of the ordinary, but then she noticed the closet door. It hung open, revealing the cavernous darkness within.

She couldn't believe she'd left it open. She always closed the closet door. It was part of her nightly ritual.

She gazed into the blackness, waiting for the face from the window to come popping out at her. She swore there was something moving around back there. She could hear it breathing, ever so faintly. It was back behind the clothes, just deep enough so she couldn't quite see.

Then, in the dead of night, it began to emerge, the face floating up out of the dark like a drowned body from the bottom of a lake. She saw those piercing eyes, the massive head, and all that hair—it covered the cheeks, nose, chin, and even the forehead.

She wanted to scream, but found she could only make a little gurgling noise in her throat. Her daddy had searched the whole room, especially the closet. How could it have hidden?

The thing stood there, just beyond the doorframe, its hairy face made silvery in the moonlight. The raspy breathing was louder now. Laticia covered her ears and tried to scream again.

The floorboards creaked as the thing stepped out of the closet. It was big and broad shouldered, and wore men's clothing. Laticia pretended to be asleep, thinking it was her only hope. Even if she managed to call for help, the thing would get her before anyone came.

She even closed her eyes, hoping it would all turn out to be one long nightmare. Then she felt the foot of her bed sink, as though someone very heavy had just sat down. She could smell foul breath. She cringed, waiting for the monster to grab her with its gnarly hands.

But it only sat there at the foot of the bed, watching her. She ventured a peek under her eyelashes, and saw its beady eyes staring back. The massive frame rose and fell with each ragged breath.

The minutes passed and seemed like hours. Still the thing sat there, the gossamer curtain falling over its freakish face like a veil. Laticia felt as though the bed, with its big canopy, was like a cage. And her monstrous jailer was only waiting for the perfect opportunity to become her executioner.

She spent the rest of the night lying rigid with fear. At long last the sun began to rise.

She hazarded a glance toward the window where an orange glow was spreading. When she looked back the hairy-faced thing was gone, as though it had never been there.

Laticia didn't mention anything to her parents. She knew they wouldn't believe a word of it. But she told her sisters all about her terror stricken night.

Tamara thought she'd simply had a nightmare, while Charise accused her of making up the whole story. But by the time they got home from school that afternoon, Laticia's sisters had completely changed their minds. They'd been unable to resist telling their friends their sister's weird story.

The kids at school already knew the stories about the spooky old house in the Garden District. And they knew what had happened in the room Laticia now called her own. It was one of those things so horrible people only spoke of it in whispers, even one hundred years after the fact.

"We know who and *what* it was you saw in your room," Tamara said.

At first Laticia thought they were teasing her, but Charise swore they were telling the truth.

"Listen," she said, in her most serious voice. "One hundred years ago this place was a boarding house. It was owned by a lady who had a son—a crazy son with a strange kind of disease. His name was Luc. She kept him locked in the basement, so he wouldn't scare the boarders. And she knew he'd scare them, cause he wasn't just crazy. He was a freak. The disease made him all hairy. His body, his hands, and especially his face, were all covered in ugly brown hair.

"For years his momma kept him hidden away, and everything was okay. But one night he got out and got into one of the rooms where a girl was sleeping."

"Do you wanna guess which room?" Tamara asked. She seemed almost gleeful.

"My room," Laticia whispered.

Her sisters nodded.

"What did he do . . . to the girl?" Laticia asked.

"He only choked the life out of her," Tamara said. "Then he stashed the body up on top of the canopy over your bed."

"He might've gotten away with it too," Charise said. "That is if the girl's stepfather hadn't walked in and caught him in the act. Then the police were called, and they took him away to be hanged."

"But I guess he came back," Tamara concluded.

Laticia had no idea what to do. She was glad her sisters finally believed her and she told them so. She also told them she had no intention of sleeping in her bedroom ever again.

"Momma's gonna have something to say about that," Charise said. "And she's never going to believe there's a hairy old ghost in your room."

"I don't care," Laticia insisted. "She can't make me stay in there. I'll climb out the window if I have to."

Laticia's sisters knew she meant what she said. But their mother was such a strict disciplinarian. Laticia had been grounded to her room, and her room was where she'd stay. So Charise thought about it a while and came up with an idea.

She went to the big junk closet, her sisters following on her heels. She opened the door and rummaged around, and eventually produced a card table, a black cloth, and several old candles.

"What's all this stuff?" Laticia asked.

Charise draped the black cloth over her head and did an imitation of a Voodoo priestess. "We need to have an exorcism," she told her sisters. "We'll drive that evil spirit right out of the house."

They set up the table in the middle of Laticia's room, and lit the candles—thirteen in all. Then they drew a pentagram and joined hands.

"What do we do now?" Tamara asked.

"We need a chant," Charise said. "Something to drive him away. Repeat after me: Luc, get out! Get out! Be gone from this house! You're not welcome! You're not wanted!"

The other girls took up the chant and repeated it for several minutes. But nothing happened, and Tamara became frustrated. "Oh, this is all a bunch of bull," she said. "There's no ghost in here. For all we know Lottie heard those stories even before we did. She could've—"

Tamara was interrupted by the sound of someone groaning. It was a miserable and agonizing cry that could only be made by a person in searing pain. But the worst part of all was the fact that the sound was undeniably coming from inside Laticia's closet.

"What was that?" Tamara asked.

The closet door flew open, the candles were blown out and the room became freezing cold.

"He's here!" Laticia cried.

"But I don't see anything," Tamara whimpered. "Where is he?"

"Don't break the circle," Charise said. "Keep chanting."

So they repeated the words over and over. "Luc, get out! Get out! Be gone from this house. You're not wanted. You're not welcome."

Soon a misshapen shape began to swirl all around them. Laticia could see the hairy face fading in and out of the blur of motion. It was twisted with fear and desperation, and a great cloud of dark vapor trailed along behind it.

"Oh, my gosh!" Tamara shouted. "What's that?"

"Don't look at it," Charise ordered. "Just keep chanting!"

"Get out! Get out, Luc! Be gone from this house," the girls repeated, their voices rising higher and higher. "You're not wanted! You're not welcome!"

And as though it couldn't take anymore, the blur of motion went streaking through the window, sending a shower of glass cascading to the driveway, some thirty feet below.

The girls ended their chant and rose from the table, their mouths agape.

"We did it!" Charise said. "He's gone."

They all gazed at the broken window. Laticia felt an incredible sense of relief. She knew there was no hiding the window from her mother, and that Mrs. Madison would go berserk when she saw it. Nevertheless, the horrible hairy-faced thing was gone. And it wasn't coming back.

Charise and Tamara offered to let her sleep in one of their rooms. But Laticia wasn't afraid anymore. Besides, she knew she needed to get used to her own bedroom. Like it or not, she'd have to sleep there until she went to college.

And as far as she knew, her room was now the only room in the house that didn't harbor a resident ghost.

As usual she turned the bathroom light on and closed the closet door. Although there wasn't anything to be afraid of anymore, she knew she wouldn't be able to sleep without completing her normal routine. She climbed into bed, feeling more at ease than she had since moving to the new house. She pulled the covers up and snuggled in.

She was just starting to drift off when she noticed the strange shape hanging above her. There was a sagging lump in the middle of the canopy, as though something large were lying on top. She stared at it, transfixed, and it began to move, wiggling its way to the edge of the canopy. Then it peeked over the edge and peered down at her.

Laticia could see it was a girl about her own age. And the girl looked fairly normal, except for the fact that she'd obviously been dead for a long time. Her face was dark blue, and there was a ring of finger-shaped bruises around her neck.

"Luc was my friend," the girl told Laticia. "He tried to protect me."

"P-p-protect you from what?" Laticia asked, not exactly comfortable with the idea of talking to a ghost.

Before the girl could answer, the bathroom light went out with a pop, and the room was cast in complete darkness.

"From him," the girl whispered, looking toward the bathroom. She was in the bed now, lying right next to Laticia. "That's my stepfather in there. He's the one who murdered me. Not Luc. Luc came and found me after it was too late. He cried over my body, while my stepfather hid in the bathroom."

Laticia thought she could see something in the bathroom mirror—movement, a dark figure.

"He hid in there 'til the police came," the girl continued. "Then he came out and told them Luc did it."

The shape in the mirror lurched suddenly, and a menacing pair of eyes gleamed in the moonlight. And Laticia suddenly realized that someone was climbing right out of the old mirror.

The blue-skinned girl whimpered and pulled the covers up over her head.

But before Laticia could react at all, a man bolted from the bathroom and flew at her like an escaped lunatic. His face was ghastly pale and bloated. He had a misshapen head and bulging bloodshot eyes. He barred his teeth like an animal and clutched at the air with his filthy hands.

"You've been telling lies again," he hissed. "You've been trying to turn your mother against me."

Laticia didn't understand his strange ranting, but it seemed as though he thought he was talking to his stepdaughter. Yet the stepdaughter's ghost had evaporated, leaving Laticia all alone.

Suddenly the horrible man lunged forward and tried to grab her. She threw herself onto the floor and rolled under the bed.

The blue-faced girl was there, waiting for her. "I used to hide under here a lot," she told Laticia. "But now there's no hiding from him. He can go anywhere."

As if to prove what the girl had said, the bloated man came slithering toward them on his belly. He looked as though he'd be too big to fit under the bed, but at the last second his stocky body stretched itself out and he came sliding in beneath the box spring. He grabbed Laticia by her ankle.

She kicked and wiggled her way free. Then she scrambled out from under the bed and made a break for the door.

The door wouldn't open. The handle wouldn't even turn. Behind her she could sense him rising up and advancing on her again.

"I'll teach you to tell lies!" he spat and scrambled for her throat.

She ducked and bolted across the room. She had no place to run, and she was running out of places to hide. Out of desperation, she threw open the closet and rushed inside. Clothes came showering down over her head.

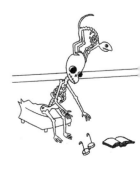

She slammed the door and gripped the doorknob as tightly as she could.

The door rattled and shook. The knob turned icy cold and twisted all around in her hands. She knew she couldn't keep him out for long. He was too strong. And she didn't hold out much hope that her family would save her. The same force that had trapped her in the bedroom would surely keep them out.

Laticia felt she had only one chance to survive the night. She closed her eyes and tried to clear her mind. Then she began to chant.

"Luc. Luc. Come back. Come back," she called. "I know you were trying to protect me. Please protect me now. Luc. Luc. Come back. Come back."

The closet door had stopped rattling, but now the bolts were popping right of their hinges. Laticia could feel the knob slipping from her sweaty fingers, as the entire door began to collapse.

The bald man stood glowering down at her, with a feverish light in his eyes. His head looked as though it had been chiseled from stone. His fingernails were caked black with filth.

Laticia was trapped. She closed her eyes and waited for the inevitable. She expected the meaty hands to close around her neck at any second.

But nothing happened.

She opened one eye and saw that the man seemed distracted with something. Then Laticia saw it too: a familiar hairy face peering in through the window.

The blue skinned girl stepped out of the shadows and threw open the sash. Luc drifted inside like a thick fog. His piercing eyes were full of anger. And those eyes were focused only in one direction.

"No," the bald ghost cried. "Not you!"

Luc barreled toward him like a locomotive. The two entities met in the middle of the room and grappled. They twisted this way and that, swirling all about in one great mass of vapor and ectoplasm. They flew up the walls and over the ceiling and back again, knocking furniture over as they went.

Laticia and the dead girl stood watching. And soon the girl began to chant. "Get out. Get out. You can't hurt me anymore. You can't hurt my friend."

Laticia joined in: "Get out! Get out! You can't hurt me anymore. You can't hurt my friend."

The mass of vapor slowed down, and Luc and the bald man became visible. Luc had a hold of him. But the man was cursing and biting. "Let go! Let go!" he growled.

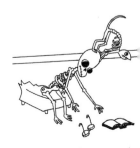

Finally he dislodged himself from Luc's grip. Then he ran and jumped back into the old mirror, disappearing in its darkened recesses.

Luc and the two girls moved toward the bathroom. Now they all took up the chant. "Get out! Get out! You can't hurt me anymore! You can't hurt any of us anymore!"

Then Luc took his great hairy fist and dashed the mirror into a million shimmering shards.

Mrs. Madison knew her daughters were up to no good. She could hear them playing at something in Laticia's room. They all three should've known better. It was a school night, and it was too late for such nonsense. She marched up the stairs and threw open the door. "What do you three think you're doing?" she shouted. "Do any of you have any idea how late . . ."

For the first time in many years Mrs. Madison was struck silent. Her three daughters were there all right, sitting on the floor and playing a board game. But the girls weren't the only ones in the room. A large man and a small girl were sitting with them. Only the man's face was covered in dark hair, and the girl's skin was a death-stricken blue.

And the pair didn't seem to be all there. One second Mrs. Madison could see them clearly, then they'd fade out, and the Monopoly houses and the "get out of jail free" card would float in midair.

Mrs. Madison, however, was never one to miss a beat. In fact, she barely batted an eye. "Okay," she told her daughters.

"I see that you all have company. But I want you in bed by twelve. After all, this is a school night."

With that she shut the door and padded back downstairs.

Laticia and her sisters looked at one another. Then they began to giggle.

And they giggled all the way to midnight.

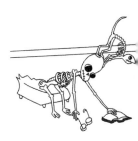

BONUS STORY

The Sacrifice

Young couples often believe their love is the work of destiny. Billy Perkins and Laura Wood were certainly no exception. And in their case, everyone who knew them agreed. The more romantic types in town all said it—there was something special about that love—something that might just keep Billy and Laura together forever.

Billy was captain of the football team, and Laura his Homecoming Queen. They started going steady their freshman year, and swore they'd get married right after graduation.

Four years came and went. Billy and Laura's senior year drifted by. Soon it was time to trade the caps and gowns of graduation for veil, wedding dress, and tux. Billy said it was like leaving the gymnasium in the middle of a dance, with the music and the laughter fading into the background. "But it's not what's back there that I care

about," he told Laura. "It's what's waiting for us, our whole lives together, that's all that matters now."

Laura was so happy she began to cry. "I'll always be with you, Billy," she promised. "We'll grow old together. Only I won't feel old, as long as I'm your wife."

Billy spent much of his senior year building a little house on a plot of land his father gave him. He even quit the football team to free up some time. His friends helped him when they could. And something slowly rose up in back of his father's fields—something that resembled a home.

Billy spent the rest of his time working at the grocery store, saving the money to buy the diamond ring. Laura worked at the movie theater, and planned the wedding right down to the color of the napkin rings.

June arrived. The sky was vast and blue and seemed to hold as many birds as there are fish in the sea. Laura picked out her dress. Billy rented his tux. They set the date. They called the preacher. They booked the band.

Then Laura came down with a fever.

No reason to postpone the wedding, her mother said. It was nothing serious. Just a slight touch of something, though the doctor wouldn't say what.

But the wedding day came and went, and there was no wedding. Laura was still sick. Billy couldn't even see her. The doctor quarantined her house, because they couldn't tell what it was she had.

They said she could only lie in bed, with a washcloth on her forehead. Her pretty green eyes were glazed over and her long brown hair was tangled. She moved in fits and starts in her feverish half-sleep. Her mother tried to soothe her with the damp cloth.

"It's going to be okay," Mrs. Wood whispered. "Soon you'll get better. Soon you'll be married."

Laura died near the end of summer, with her mother at her bedside, and Billy two miles away. He was putting the finishing touches on the house that was to be their home. The preacher and Billy's father rode out to break the news.

Billy sat down right there on the floor of the new house and didn't say a word. Nothing the preacher or his father said could make him stir.

At the funeral they kept the casket closed. The doctor never did figure out what killed Laura, and they weren't taking any chances.

Laura's mother cried. Billy's mother cried. But Billy just stood there in stunned silence. It had all happened so quickly. Now the preacher was through and they were lowering the casket into the clay. Billy felt like an empty shell. He wished he were in the coffin too, stone dead and down in the pitch darkness beside his beloved.

Later that night he lay on his bed and stared at the darkened ceiling. He was exhausted, but he didn't feel much like sleeping. Eventually he lapsed into a kind of half-sleep, but the train woke him at midnight.

First it was just a little humming way off in the night. Then the horn blew, mournful and distant. Billy didn't think much of it. He'd heard

trains before. He lay there and listened to the rolling, rattling shuffle. Then the horn sounded again, louder this time, and he remembered that the nearest train tracks were miles and miles away.

How could there be a train passing through his father's fields?

He climbed out of bed and into his jeans. He opened the window and leaned on the sill.

The train was coming closer, all right. The very ground seemed to shuffle and shake. And there was no mistaking that horn. It sounded fat and as mournful as the night.

Then he saw her—a girl drifting, almost gliding, through the wheat field. His heart pounded like a kettledrum. He swung his legs over the windowsill and leapt to the ground.

The girl had disappeared.

Billy ran across the yard and thrashed his way into the wheat. He couldn't see her, but he knew she was still there. He peered over the tops of the sheaves and saw the train passing the field, a big black shape rolling on into the darkness.

Then he saw her again. She was up at the head of the field, very near the train. She was walking straight toward it, like she meant to climb on board.

Billy couldn't see her face, but he knew. He simply knew.

"Laura!" he cried. "Don't go! Wait for me!"

She turned around, and he saw her face. Laura was as beautiful as he'd ever seen her. Her eyes were as clear as the Caribbean Sea. Her lips were full, her cheeks lush with life.

She was waiting for him. She couldn't bear to be without him. He knew just how she felt. He waded through the wheat, fighting his way toward her. But as he drew closer the train passed on and disappeared into the night. The horn died away and the ground grew still.

And so went Laura, fading into the field like a wood sprite. Billy thrashed all around, frantically searching the spot where she'd vanished. But Laura was gone.

Billy gave up and sank down in the middle of the field. He'd lost his love a second time, yet he wasn't without hope.

She hadn't boarded the train. She chose instead to wait for him. Maybe, Billy thought, just maybe, we'll meet again.

The next morning Billy told his parents what he'd seen. Of course they both said it was all just a dream.

"No, it wasn't," Billy swore. "I know what I saw. It was real. It was Laura."

His parents didn't try to argue with him much. Instead they ate their breakfast in silence.

Later his father took him aside. "Look, son, I know what you thought you saw. And, who knows, maybe you did see Laura. Stranger things have happened."

Billy was only half listening.

"But what you have got to remember," his father urged. "Is that things don't stay the same way forever. It's not fair that you and Laura had so little time together, but you can't go back, son. Things just can't be the way they were, not ever again. Laura's gone."

Billy simply couldn't accept what his father said. And he found he couldn't sleep at all that night. He wandered all around the farm, eventually wending his way to the plot of land where he'd built the house.

He stood staring up at the white porch, the oak front door, and the gabled second-story windows. That's when he heard the train again—the distant shuffling, the melancholy horn.

Then Laura was there, standing in front of the second-story window and gazing down at him. Her face was pale and pretty. Her green eyes were mournful and seemed to beg him to come closer.

Billy ran across the little yard and burst through the front door. He hurtled up the stairs, his pulse pounding. But he found no sign of Laura. The house was as deserted as ever, and when he called her name his voice echoed through the empty rooms.

He stood in the exact spot where she'd been standing. He gazed out through the same window.

The wheat field looked like an ocean under the pale moonlight. And when the wind blew through the sheaves they seemed to crash like waves.

The train was coming closer too. He could feel the earth rumble as the big iron wheels rolled over the rails. Yet he knew there were no rails—not for miles around—and there could be no train coming through his father's fields. It didn't make sense.

But he forgot all about what did and didn't make sense when he saw Laura. She was standing at the edge of the field, watching him. The wind whipped her brown hair all around her shoulders.

She was waiting for him. She wanted him to go with her—he could feel it. He knew she couldn't bear to go away and leave him behind.

"Wait, Laura! Wait!" he yelled, almost falling down the stairs and stumbling out into the yard. "I don't want to live without you!"

And he meant what he said. He was prepared to die, rather than be left all alone.

Laura was moving across the field, but she kept looking back over her shoulder. She wanted him to catch up. She wanted to take him with her. He could sense it.

He saw the train off in the distance. It was like an endless iron serpent, twisting and turning its way over the countryside. A great billowing cloud of smoke rose up from the stacks. As Billy drew closer he could see inside the windows. Thick red curtains obstructed much of the view, but between these he saw pale shapes floating in a soft light. One by one their blue faces bobbed in front of the windows and they gazed out over the countryside with lonesome eyes.

Many of these faces seemed familiar to Billy. He swore he'd seen them in photographs hanging on the walls of his neighbor's houses and in the halls of his school.

Laura was halfway across the field now. Billy was two hundred yards behind her. The sheaves of wheat seemed to part before her as if

she were a gale of wind. Billy ran as hard as he could, shouting her name at the top of his lungs.

She stopped in front of the train and turned, waiting. Waiting for him as she'd done the night before. But Billy was too slow. The train vanished once more, and Laura faded into thin air.

Still she hadn't boarded the train. Billy knew he had at least one more chance to be reunited with his love. He'd wait. He'd sit right down in the field and wait the next night until the train came rattling toward his father's farm and Laura returned to him once and for all.

Billy's father found him kneeling in the field at dawn. Both his parents were very worried. They called the doctor, but the doctor said there wasn't anything wrong with Billy that medicine could cure. So they called the preacher. He drove out in his old black car, the dust trailing in its wake. He stood in front of Billy in his old black coat, clutching a Bible in his hand. "What's troubling you, son?" he asked.

"It's Laura," Billy said. "I've seen her two nights in a row, Reverend. She walks across the field toward a train, like she wants to get on board. I call her and sometimes she looks back. I think she wants me to go with her, to get on the train with her."

"Boy," the preacher said. "You listen to me and listen good. Don't go anywhere near that train. And if you see Laura again, don't you go near her either."

"But why?" Billy demanded.

"That's not Laura you're seeing," the preacher explained. "That's her shade—her wandering spirit. And that train's coming to carry her over to the other side. She's gotta get onboard without hesitation and with no regrets. Because if she has regret in her heart, she'll ride forever, trapped between the two worlds."

"Well, Laura's only regret would be leaving me behind," said Billy.

The preacher shook his head. "If you get on that train you'll go too—long before your rightful time."

"That's fine by me," Billy said. "I don't have any reason to live. Not without Laura."

The preacher waved his Bible inches in front of Billy's nose. "You young fool," he shouted. "Don't you understand? A man can't just choose to go. Not before his rightful time. It's a sin. And if Laura's trying to take you with her that makes her evil, boy. A harpie. A wraith. And you had better stay away."

"Don't you talk about her that way!" Billy screamed. "I don't care what you say! I'll make any sacrifice to be with Laura again!"

Billy stormed out of the house, oblivious to his parents' pleas. He ran and hid in the field. His mother and father called and called, but he ignored them, and eventually they had to give up. He settled in among the wheat and waited for nightfall.

He must have drifted off to sleep. The train woke him with a start. It was already on top of the farm, barreling downhill toward the edge of

the field. The entire landscape shuddered as the huge engine devoured a ton of coal and kept the pistons churning in a blur of perpetual motion. The iron wheels ground on and on, sending blue sparks shooting up from rails that hadn't existed only hours before.

Then he saw her. She was a few yards in front of him, her green eyes peering out from between the sheaves of wheat. He called to her, and she opened her mouth to respond, but her words were drowned as the horn sounded. The great noise echoed across the countryside like the death cry of some prehistoric beast. It was so loud it made Billy cover his ears and sent him sinking to his knees.

By the time he recovered himself, Laura was moving on toward the train. He started after her, calling. She turned her head and looked back, as if to say "Hurry. Hurry, before it's too late."

Billy ran as hard as his legs could carry him. Laura was only a few dozen yards ahead now, but she was getting closer to the train—which seemed to be slowing at last. The grinding wheels began to whine, as if the brakeman had thrown the switch.

A porter, dressed all in black, opened one of the cars from the inside and swung himself out into the wind. His face was as white as an eggshell, his teeth as yellow as the yolk. He clung to the railing with one hand and extended the other out toward Laura.

Laura was very close to the train now. She was climbing the ridge that led up to the mysterious tracks. Billy was afraid he wouldn't catch her after all, so he let out one last desperate yelp.

"Laura! Please wait!"

She heard him. She stopped and turned around. Billy could see that she was sad. Laura looked as lonely as Rapunzel stuck way up in her tower. She would take him with her. It had to be. Without her, Billy had no desire to live.

But just as he was close enough to grab her, she shook her head. Billy was stunned. And when Laura turned and took the porter's hand and was swept aboard the train, he couldn't believe it. He wouldn't believe it.

He kept running. She watched him from the open car of the train, her face so pretty, unblemished, and pure. He ran ever harder, his lungs almost bursting. He had to catch up. He would be with her at any cost.

The train was moving faster now—pistons plunging, wheels rolling, smoke rising. Billy was only a few feet from Laura's car. He reached out, made a desperate lunge, and caught a hold of the railing.

Grinning, he pulled himself aboard, eager to receive her welcoming kiss.

But Laura's only welcome was a troubled frown. And as she shook her head her face began to change. The flush faded rapidly from her cheeks, which grew wan and sunken until horrid black pits were all that remained. Then rivers of decay spread out from her mouth, causing her flesh to shrivel and fall away. Billy could see her skull, covered now only by a putrid slime. Her

brown hair had fallen out of her head. Even her clothes were coming apart, exposing the rotting skeleton beneath.

Billy fell into a faint, losing his grip on the railing, and landing with a thud on the hard earth. He rolled back into his father's field, and clung to the ground. He'd seen the horrible face of death. It was unlike anything he'd imagined, and now he knew he wanted no part of it. Now he knew he wanted nothing more than to live—to breathe clean air and eat good food, and do all of the things that only the living can do.

He pulled himself to his feet. The train was thundering on, climbing out of the field and heading for the horizon. Billy saw Laura, standing at the railing, her beauty completely restored.

Then it dawned on him. She had wanted him to go with her. She didn't want to be alone any more than he did. But at the last minute she found she couldn't let him make that sacrifice. Although her desire for him was great, her desire that he should live was even greater.

So she had to show him. Show him what it was like to die, so he'd have the will to keep on living.

Laura was the one who'd sacrificed after all. Now Billy watched her as the train disappeared over the horizon. Her green eyes gazed back through the darkness, as if through the veil of many years. She looked very pretty and so very alone. But Billy knew she was going to the other side without hesitation, and with a heart that held not a single regret.